To John, Samantha, Natalee, and Leslie,
for believing in this world,
and
to Patty and Emily,
for everything else

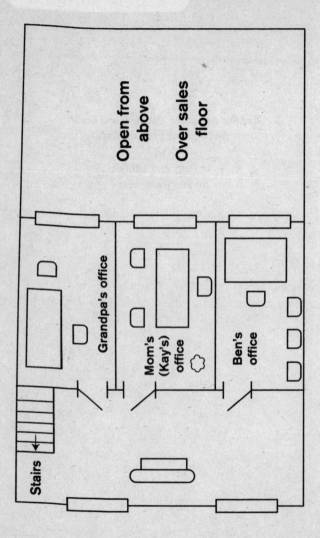

Stairs

Grandpa's office

Mom's
(Kay's)
office

Ben's
office

Open from
above

Over sales
floor

Praise for Tim Myers' Candlemaking Mystery series

Snuffed Out

"A sure winner." —Carolyn Hart,
author of the Death on Demand series

"An interesting mystery, a large cast of characters, and an engaging amateur sleuth make this series a winner."
—*The Romance Reader's Connection* (four daggers)

At Wick's End

"A smashing, successful debut." —*Midwest Book Review*

"I greatly enjoyed this terrific mystery. The main character . . . will make you laugh. Don't miss this thrilling read."
—*Rendezvous*

"A clever and well done debut." —*Mysterylovers*

Praise for Tim Myers' Lighthouse Mystery series

"A thoroughly delightful and original series. Book me at Hatteras West any day!" —Tamar Myers,
author of *Thou Shalt Not Grill*

"Myers cultivates the North Carolina scenery with aplomb and shows a flair for character." —*Fort Lauderdale Sun-Sentinel*

"Entertaining . . . authentic . . . fun . . . a wonderful regional mystery that will have readers rebooking for future stays at the Hatteras West Inn and Lighthouse." —*BookBrowser*

"Tim Myers proves that he is no one-book wonder . . . A shrewdly crafted puzzle." —*Midwest Book Review*

"Colorful . . . picturesque . . . light and entertaining."
—*The Best Reviews*

DEAD MEN DON'T LYE

TIM MYERS

PB
Myers

BERKLEY PRIME CRIME, NEW YORK

THE BERKLEY PUBLISHING GROUP
Published by the Penguin Group
Penguin Group (USA) Inc.
375 Hudson Street, New York, New York 10014, USA
Penguin Group (Canada), 90 Eglinton Avenue East, Suite 700, Toronto, Ontario M4P 2Y3, Canada
(a division of Pearson Penguin Canada Inc.)
Penguin Books Ltd., 80 Strand, London WC2R 0RL, England
Penguin Group Ireland, 25 St. Stephen's Green, Dublin 2, Ireland (a division of Penguin Books Ltd.)
Penguin Group (Australia), 250 Camberwell Road, Camberwell, Victoria 3124, Australia
(a division of Pearson Australia Group Pty. Ltd.)
Penguin Books India Pvt. Ltd., 11 Community Centre, Panchsheel Park, New Delhi—110 017,
India
Penguin Group (NZ), Cnr. Airborne and Rosedale Roads, Albany, Auckland 1310, New Zealand
(a division of Pearson New Zealand Ltd.)
Penguin Books (South Africa) (Pty.) Ltd., 24 Sturdee Avenue, Rosebank, Johannesburg 2196, South
Africa

Penguin Books Ltd., Registered Offices: 80 Strand, London WC2R 0RL, England

This is a work of fiction. Names, characters, places, and incidents either are the product of the author's imagination or are used fictitiously, and any resemblance to actual persons, living or dead,
business establishments, events, or locales is entirely coincidental. The publisher does not have
any control over and does not assume any responsibility for author or third-party websites or their
content.

DEAD MEN DON'T LYE

A Berkley Prime Crime Book / published by arrangement with the author

PRINTING HISTORY
Berkley Prime Crime mass-market edition / February 2006

ISBN: 0-425-20744-7

BERKLEY® PRIME CRIME
Berkley Prime Crime Books are published by The Berkley Publishing Group,
a division of Penguin Group (USA) Inc.,
375 Hudson Street, New York, New York 10014.
The name BERKLEY PRIME CRIME and the BERKLEY PRIME CRIME design are trademarks
belonging to Penguin Group (USA) Inc.

PRINTED IN THE UNITED STATES OF AMERICA

10 9 8 7 6 5 4 3 2 1

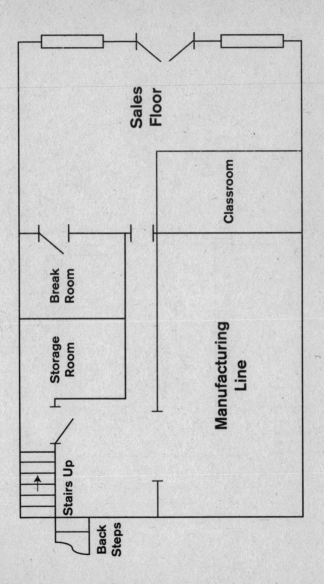

ONE

∘ ∘ ∘

AS I looked down at the corpse sprawled on the back steps of my family's soap shop and boutique, I knew in an instant there wasn't a cleanser made anywhere in the world strong enough to get rid of the acid stains and burns on Jerry Sanger's face. Believe me, if there had been, I would have known about it. My name's Benjamin Perkins, and along with a family sporting a larger population than some small countries, I run Where There's Soap. We specialize in soap in all its many incarnations. We've got it all, from small production runs in back to the sales boutique storefront filled with products our entire family creates. We give group and individual lessons in the art of soapmaking in our classroom, a handsome source of income for the business. In addition to all that, we sell kits, supplies, and everything else a hobbyist soapmaker could possibly want.

At one time the family business had actually been a full-scale soap factory, started by my great-grandfather

Martin—a man I remembered most for the peppermint smell that always clung to his clothes—but over the years we've scaled back our main production line to focus on individual customers up front, too. Our family's a nice blend, with each member having their own area of expertise. What's mine? Besides filling in wherever I'm needed, it's up to me to fix whatever goes wrong, and believe me, with the family and the business, I am never bored.

As I studied the body on the steps, I thought about how my sister Louisa was going to react. She'd been dating Jerry lately, and it was going to be an ugly scene when she found out he was dead. I'd have to deal with her later, though. At the moment, I tried to think if there was anything I could do besides call the police. I'd always felt like some kind of big, clumsy oaf next to Jerry—he was seven inches shorter than my six feet, and he weighed a good thirty pounds less than my 180. He had been a cocky little bantam of a man, and if I was being honest, I'd have to admit that I never really cared for him.

Even though Jerry was long past any help I could give him, I leaned down and checked for a pulse anyway, being careful not to get any acid on my hands. The lye's identification was unmistakable from its odor, though I doubted that had been what killed him. The weird cant of his neck was enough to explain how he'd probably died. Whether the splashes of lye had come before or after his demise was the coroner's business, not mine. Before the lye, Jerry had been a handsome fellow, a little too attractive for his own good, in my opinion. He was especially proud of his hair. While mine was plain brown with whispers of gray coming in at the temples, I'd long suspected that Jerry's was a shade of chestnut that had to come from a bottle or a stylist.

None of that really mattered now, and I found myself regretting the verbal jabs I'd taken at him in the past. Someone had killed him, doused him in lye, and then had the nerve to dump the body on our back doorstep. The fact that Jerry was more than just the supplier who brought us the liquids and scents we used for soapmaking—including the acid he was currently soaked in—just made matters worse. I'd warned my sister about him but, as always, Louisa had chosen to ignore my excellent advice. At least most of the rest of my six siblings listened to me. Occasionally. When it suited them.

I had just confirmed that that particular relationship wouldn't be going any further when I heard a gasp behind me. "Don't let it be Louisa," I said under my breath as I started to turn around.

It wasn't Louisa. It was infinitely worse. My mother stood in the doorway with the saddest look in her eyes I'd ever seen. As slim as my sister Cindy, her hair had been frosted platinum for so long that no one remembered its original color.

"I know you two didn't get along, but did you have to kill him, Benjamin?"

That was classic Mom, prone to exaggeration and one of the best conclusion-jumpers around. "Come on, Mom, you know better than that. I just found him like this two minutes ago."

My mother fanned herself with her apron, a habit of hers that signified she was really stressed out. Well, she had every right to be. I caught a glimpse of the nice print dress underneath. Mom was a big fan of aprons, and for Christmas one year as a gag, all seven of us—her kids ranging from Cindy at eighteen all the way up to me at thirty-three—bought her the exact same apron. We'd been expecting laughter; instead, she dutifully rotated the aprons at work, one for each day of the week, after carefully stitching each donor's name on the tag. At the rate she was wearing them, the aprons would outlive us all.

Her frown intensified as she stared down at the body.

"Give me some credit, Benjamin; I know you didn't kill Mr. Sanger." She looked away from the body, then added, "Your sister must not see this."

"See what?" Louisa asked from behind her. She had always been plain-looking, her hair never as shiny as Kate's nor her figure as petite as Cindy's. On top of all that, she'd been the only girl to inherit the Perkins nose, and while it looked all right on Jeff and Grandpa, it hadn't done her any favors. She'd overcompensated with a sarcastic wit that could snap with the best of them, and I'd always admired her for her intelligence and strength of will.

"Take her inside, Mom," I said forcefully, trying to block my sister's view of the body.

Louisa spotted her late beau despite my efforts. I wasn't sure what I was expecting, but her initial reaction surprised me, and I've known her all her life. "I'd be lying if I said I wasn't thinking about doing something just like that myself," she said. The callousness of her words suddenly struck her, then she started to cry. "Oh, Mamma."

As Louisa buried her head into our mother's shoulder, I said, "I thought you two were still dating."

Louisa explained through her tears. "We were, until I found out he had at least two other girlfriends on his route, and that's just in this part of North Carolina."

"When did this happen?" I asked.

"I got an anonymous telephone call early this morning from one of the other women. She didn't have the courage to leave her name, but there was no doubt in my mind she was telling the truth. He actually told me I was the only one in his heart." She buried her face in Mom's shoulder again.

I reached for my cell phone, and Mom asked, "Benjamin, who are you calling at a time like this?"

"I'm dialing 911," I said. "We have to tell the police."

Mom nodded. "Of course, you're right. It's the proper thing to do. Benjamin, you deal with them when they come."

Though my mother had seniority in the company and acted as our CEO, she usually left the sticky situations for me to handle. Those duties—along with occasionally teaching classes up front and helping the guys out on the production line—managed to keep me hopping all the time. Dad had done the same thing before me, but he'd been killed five years ago when a delivery truck had run him down in our own alley. I was the oldest child, the next in the line of seniority, and I had inherited his headaches dealing with the family's problems. Grandpa was mostly retired, handling advertising when he wasn't off traveling somewhere, while Mom made the executive decisions. My sisters ran the storefront, and my brothers handled the factory end of it; I had somehow been pegged as the family and business troubleshooter. Whenever there was a problem with any part of the business or the Perkins clan, it ended up squarely in my lap. With as many lives as that description touched, I was always putting a fire out somewhere.

Before I dialed the second "one" of the emergency number, I hung up and dialed another number from memory. When the desk sergeant answered, I asked for Molly Wilkes, a girl I'd dated off and on since high school. She had shocked us all upon graduation by going into the police academy, and she'd become a darned good cop along the way. Luckily she was at her desk.

"Hi, Molly, it's Ben."

She hesitated on the other end of the line. "Ben? Nope, doesn't ring any bells. I was supposed to have dinner with an old boyfriend named Ben, but he stood me up last week. I'm really sorry, but I don't know anybody by that name anymore."

"Come on, I already apologized for that. I had a flat tire and my cell phone battery was dead, so I couldn't call you," I said.

"A likely story."

"Listen Molly, I've got some trouble at Where There's Soap, and I need your help."

The banter ended abruptly. "What's going on?"

"One of my suppliers is dead on my back steps."

"Heart attack?" she asked.

"Not unless he died of fright when somebody threw liquid lye on him and gave him a shove off the landing." I thought about how the body lay, the staged look of it. "You know what? I'm starting to think he wasn't killed here." I took a deep breath and tried to stop rambling. "It's not pretty."

"Don't touch anything. I'll be right there."

I hung up, then turned to the women at the top of the stairs. "Mom, why don't you take Louisa inside? She'd probably like to be with Cindy and Kate." My sisters had a support group that rivaled any in the world.

Mom nodded, then said, "Aren't you coming in, too?"

"No, I'm going to wait out here for Molly."

Mom nodded, then crossed herself as she glanced at the corpse again before leading Louisa back into the shop.

I stayed put to keep Jerry company. It had been the start of a beautiful summer day like we sometimes enjoyed in our part of North Carolina—not too hot, yet with the sun shining brightly and the birds in full voice—but it was cold and overcast in my soul. I didn't need Molly to tell me how this was going to look to the police. Mom had been right in the spirit of her first statement; the supplier and I hadn't gotten along very well. While I'd never suspected he'd been three-timing my sister, there had been something just a little too smooth about the man since he'd taken over our route. The two of us had words about his sloppy work habits the week before, and I'd said some things I would have liked to take back, but it was too late for that now. So who would kill him? Louisa didn't even cross my mind as a suspect. She'd once taken a *D* in science class in high school, refusing to cut open a frog on moral principles, and I couldn't see my sister—no matter how scorned she was— killing Jerry, regardless of her blunt admission that she'd been ready to murder him herself.

Molly drove up three minutes later, her lights and siren mute. That was one good thing about living in a small town like Harper's Landing. No one was ever that far away. She was being thoughtful with her silent approach, no doubt realizing that the shop didn't need that kind of publicity, and acknowledging that a fuss wasn't going to do Jerry a bit of good. When she got out of the squad car, I noticed that Molly's long lustrous black hair was pulled back into a tight bun to make her look more professional, but not even the standard-issue uniform could disguise her ample curves. Though Molly constantly complained about wanting to lose fifteen pounds, she had always looked great to me; I was never a big fan of bony women. What drew me to her most though was the constant glint in her brown eyes, a spark that always danced in the light. Molly and I were friends who sometimes dated, an odd relationship we'd worked out over the years. It left us free to see other people whenever we wanted, but also provided some stability in our lives, a safe port for each of us. Mom still had delusions that someday we'd both wake up and realize we were in love, no matter how much Molly and I protested to the contrary.

Molly nodded once to me, leaned down to check the body for a pulse, then obviously came to the same conclusion I had. "Did you touch anything?" she asked.

"Just his neck when I was looking for a pulse myself. I didn't change the angle of his head, though. He was like that when I found him. Be careful, that lye is caustic."

"You use lye in your shop, don't you?"

"It's tough to make soap without it," I said. "Jerry supplied our liquid and pellet lye, along with a ton of other things we use here."

"Educate me, Ben. It's an acid, I know that much."

I nodded. "It's not only that, it's a poison, too. Lye can be really nasty stuff."

"And it's in soap? Wonderful."

I shook my head. "It's not actually in the soap, it's an intermediate, and if you use it correctly, it's entirely consumed by the oils and fats as you're processing. The stuff is cheap, it's convenient, and if you're careful, it's safe enough."

"Somebody wasn't all that concerned about being careful with it here, were they?" she said. Molly pointed to my shoes. "You've been up and down these steps, haven't you?"

"Just the ones above," I said. "I had to see if he was still alive, didn't I?"

She nodded. "Okay. The forensics team is right behind me." To prove her words, a van drove up and parked behind her cruiser. Molly said, "Why don't you go back inside? I'll be there in a few minutes to talk to you."

"There's something urgent we need to discuss. Molly, it's important." I had to tell her about my sister's relationship with the victim before she heard it from someone else.

"Let me get them started, then I'll be in soon. I promise."

I went back inside to find my entire family waiting for me. It was a grand inquisition that few suitors had been able to face over the years, though Bob and Kate had somehow found spouses willing to put up with all of us. Neither of their partners had expressed any desire to join the family business though, a decision Mom had heartily approved. I couldn't blame them; I'd been born into the family, and I sometimes found the Perkins clan a little too much to take myself.

They all started talking at once, pelting me with more questions than I could possibly answer. I ignored them all and looked around the building, waiting for everyone to calm down long enough to let me speak. We were in the back where the production line was. There were no fancy faux finishes on the walls here, though the space did share the same heavily patinaed floor that the boutique section had. The wood had been there as long as the building, and I loved the character it brought to the place. I could see through the open connecting door that the lights of the shop were on, and I wondered if the front door was still locked. There were shelves stocked with soaps that ranged from the simplest to the most complex offerings possible, and I caught a glimpse of the crafters section, brimming with supplies, molds, and accessories.

It was pretty obvious they weren't going to shut up on their own. I held up my hands and they finally quieted. "Here's how things stand right now. Jerry Sanger is dead. It looks like whoever did it broke his neck and splashed him with lye. That's all I know. Molly will be in as soon as she can."

I should have known that wouldn't satisfy any of them. Cindy and Kate were on either side of Louisa, offering more than just moral support. It appeared that the two of them were holding her up. All three of my brothers—Jim, Bob, and Jeff—were standing at the windows watching the techs work up the crime scene. Jim, the second son and third child, said, "It looks like somebody beat us to it. That guy got just what he deserved." He was quite a bit huskier than I was, more solid and stronger as well, my "little" brother in name only.

At his pronouncement, Louisa started crying again, and my other sisters led her back to our break room.

Mom shot Jim a frown before joining them.

Bob patted Jim's shoulder. "Nice going, Bro. You missed your calling; you should have joined the diplomatic corps." Bob was the style rebel of our crew, his hair grown long and pulled back into a ponytail. His wife Jessica was constantly trying to get him to cut it, but my otherwise easygoing brother had flatly refused. He considered himself the artist of the family, and he wasn't about to change his appearance.

"Are you trying to tell me you weren't thinking the same thing?"

Jeff, my youngest brother, said, "Come on guys, we need to stick together on this. Ben, what do you think?" Jeff had a slight frame and unfortunately was starting to lose his hair. He was the dreamer of our clan, the positive spirit who constantly sought to buoy the rest of us.

"I think we should let Molly handle it. She's not going to suspect Louisa. She's known her all her life."

Jim said, "You're dreaming. We all know she had every reason to do it."

Bob said, "Hey, whose side are you on, anyway?"

Jim started for the door. "I'm on the family's side, where else would I be? I'm going to see what's going on for myself."

This had the potential to get ugly fast. One of my roles since the others had come along was to act as peacemaker, no matter how conflicted I felt myself. I put a hand on my brother Jim's chest. If he really wanted to get past me, I wasn't sure I could stop him. "Guys, let's take it easy, okay? We need to let Molly do her job." Jim started to protest, but I cut him off. "I don't care what any of us think; we've got to present a united front here. Quiet down, here comes Molly."

She'd circled the building and came in the front door, then offered her greeting to my brothers. Molly Wilkes had been a part of my life for so long she was an honorary member of the family. "Can I talk to you alone, Ben?"

"Why can't we stay?" Jim asked.

Bob took his arm. "Because we've got a problem with the line, and I can't fix it without your bumbling help."

Jeff said, "Come on guys, let's go. We'll leave you two

alone." His gaze lingered on Molly. It was obvious my baby brother still had a crush on her, but he felt like she was out of his league, so he'd never asked her out. It didn't keep him from pining away for her, though.

After they were gone, Molly said, "I've got to be honest with you, Ben, this doesn't look good."

"What are you talking about? You can't possibly think one of us had anything to do with this."

She shrugged. "Ben, I've known Louisa almost as long as I've known you. It's no secret she was dating the victim, I saw them together at Falling River last weekend having dinner. Ordinarily I'd say there was no way she could have done this, but your sister's had a tendency to overreact in the past when it's involved love."

"What are you talking about?"

"Ernestine Gentry," she said softly.

"You're bringing something up that happened in high school?" I asked. "That was fifteen years ago."

Molly said, "She pushed her down the steps to the gym when Ernestine stole Kyle Medford from her."

"That wasn't Louisa's fault. Ernestine tripped over her own feet. She was the biggest klutz in school."

"Then why did they suspend Louisa?"

I took a deep breath, trying to control my temper. "You know full well that Jack Gentry owned half of Harper's Landing back then. He wanted blood, and Principal Boggess gave it to him."

"It's a pattern, Ben; that's all I'm saying." Molly stared at her polished black shoes, refusing to meet my gaze.

"What is it?" I asked. "There's something else you're not telling me."

Molly said, "I should probably learn to keep my mouth shut, but I guess you have a right to know. There were splashes of lye on the upper steps, but not on the lower ones. We need to examine Louisa's clothes."

"So, what does that matter? Oh my word," I added as the meaning struck home. "Whoever doused him did it from above, from the back doorway of the shop."

"That's how it looks to us," Molly agreed. "I'm afraid I need to speak with Louisa right now."

"She's in the break room with the other women."

Molly would have probably rather faced a gun-toting robber at the moment than the women in my family, but I wasn't going to make it any easier for her.

When I didn't offer to summon my sister, Molly said reluctantly, "I'll go get her."

I followed her to the break room, a family gathering spot littered with easy chairs and a worn sofa. The best part was that it was always stocked with cookies, cakes, and pies that Mom provided. I had to walk four miles every morning before the shop opened just to hold my weight down. I can turn my nose up at the most elegant torte or mousse, but when it comes to my mother's baked goods, I have no will of my own.

I couldn't make Molly face the four women in there by herself, no matter how angry I was that my sister was her main suspect. I stopped her at the door and said, "Why don't you let me get her for you?"

Molly's look of relief was thanks enough.

I stepped inside and called to Louisa, "Come here, Sis. Molly needs to talk to you."

Louisa clutched the handkerchief in her hand tightly, but Mom put a restraining hand on her arm. "She's in no condition to talk to the police, Benjamin, even if it is Molly. Tell her I said so."

I wasn't about to add an obstruction of justice charge into the mix. "Mom, Molly has every right to speak with her. It's her job."

My mother frowned, then said, "Yes, but she's got to understand; we're family."

"That doesn't matter right now. Come on, Louisa."

Cindy and Kate started to follow. I added, "Just Louisa, ladies."

Mom nodded to the girls. "You two open the shop. We can't let our customers down. They're counting on us."

Cindy asked, "We're really opening after this happened?"

"We can't do anyone any good by keeping our doors bolted. Now do as I say." Mom turned to me and added, "Benjamin, you'll stay with Louisa, yes?"

"I'll do what I can," I agreed, wondering how I was going to sell that to Molly. Truthfully, being beside Louisa was exactly where I wanted to be. As much as I loved my sister—she was born eleven months after me and we'd been close from the start—she had a tendency to speak first and consider the consequences later. It was a trait that could get her into more trouble now than she'd ever had in her life.

It was clear Molly was not happy about my presence as Louisa and I walked out of the break room together. "I need to speak to her alone, Ben," she said.

I started to protest, but Louisa touched my arm lightly and said, "It's okay, Ben, I'll be fine."

"You shouldn't say a word unless you're with me or our lawyer," I said firmly. Harry McCallister handled our corporate account, but I doubted the aging barrister had any experience in criminal cases. I had an ace in the hole, though. An attorney named Kelly Sheer was a soapmaking enthusiast, and a new convert at that. She'd taken nearly every class we offered at Where There's Soap in the past few months. She also happened to be a big-gun lawyer from Charlotte who'd moved to Harper's Landing to raise her daughter after a bitter divorce. Kelly had offered her services a few times in jest, but I could see that she'd been serious beneath the smile, and I knew I could count on her.

Molly said, "You know, it might not be a bad idea to call

your attorney." She turned to Louisa and said, "Are you ready to go?"

"Where are we going? I don't have to look at the body again, do I?" The prospect clearly intimidated my sister.

"No, but the only way we're going to get through this is if we do the interview in my office. We need to examine your clothes, too, so you might want to get one of your sisters to meet us downtown so you'll have something to wear home."

"That's going to have to wait," I said. "I'm calling Kelly Sheer first."

Molly's eyebrows arched. "Do you know her? I didn't realize you traveled in such rarified circles, Ben."

"When it comes to my family, only the best will do."

Molly nodded. "I don't blame you a bit. I understand completely."

After they were gone, I called Kelly at her office. She readily agreed to head over to the sheriff's department and represent my sister. There was no doubt Louisa needed her, for moral support if nothing else. At least I hoped that was the only reason Kelly's presence would be required. Despite my feelings for my sister, I had to acknowledge the fact that she was Molly's prime suspect for a very good reason.

I just hoped there was no lye on Louisa's shoes or clothing. Things were bleak enough as they stood without anyone throwing gasoline onto the fire.

Two

. . .

AS soon as Louisa and Molly left, Mom started grilling me near the front registers. "You didn't go with your sister? Benjamin, what's wrong with you? You need to be there."

"Easy, Mom, I called Kelly Sheer. She can do more for Louisa than I can."

That mollified her instantly; she was a big fan of Kelly's. Mom patted my cheek as she said, "That was the smart thing to do. That's why you handle such things. So, do you know what you should be doing right now?"

"Helping the guys fix the production line?" I asked, hoping against hope that she'd say yes.

She waved a hand in the air. "Benjamin, leave the mechanical problems to your brothers. You have more important things to do."

"Is that the CEO talking, or my mother?"

Her lips pinched together for a second before she spoke. "It's both of us, smart boy."

I waited patiently for her to fill in the blanks, then I shook my head the second I realized her intent. "No way, Mom, I'm not going to do it, so don't even go there."

"Go where?" she asked innocently.

"It's Molly's job to investigate this, not mine."

Mom looked pleased with herself that I had come to the right conclusion, despite my protests. She asked pointedly, "And where is Molly now?"

I reluctantly admitted, "She's questioning Louisa downtown."

Mom nodded her head in agreement. "So if she's focusing on your sister, how is she going to catch the real killer? Answer me that."

"I wouldn't even know where to begin," I said. "I handle missing wallets and rude customers. On occasion I track down a waylaid order or an AWOL vendor, but I've never investigated a murder before."

Mom said, "I have faith in you, Benjamin. You always were clever in figuring such things out. Do you think the family will rest until Louisa's name is cleared? Will any of us sleep at night, knowing this cloud hangs over your sister's head? You must realize we'd rather have you working to clear Louisa's good name than working with us here. Do this, with all our blessings."

There was a time to stand up and fight, and there was a time to give in. Since I knew I'd already lost this battle before it started, I did the only thing I could do; I agreed. "I'm still going to teach my class, but I guess I could snoop around some and see if I can come up with anything in the meantime."

She patted my cheek, then gave it a little tweak. Depending on how she felt, Mom could make her pinch a gentle caress, or take off some skin. "You're a good son. Now get out of here and find out who really killed the late Mr. Sanger."

I walked out the front door around the building to where our cars were parked in back. One reason I chose the long route was because the forensics team might still be working the back stairs, but the more pressing reason was that I was in no hurry to go through the gauntlet of my siblings. The gardens in front were beautiful, carefully tended for more reasons than aesthetic ones. There were sections in the five-starred grid where we grew lavender, rosemary, sage, and a dozen other herbs for our soapmaking.

When I got to our parking area in back, I was happy to see that the police van was gone. I wondered what they might have found there, and if Molly would share the information with me. It was going to be a delicate situation digging into this while Molly was investigating, but Mom was right. I couldn't just leave Louisa's fate in anyone else's hands. I got into my emerald green Miata, still not clear as to what I should be doing. I didn't know Jerry Sanger all that well, so I couldn't exactly check out his haunts or his house. That was Molly's job, and I wondered how I should begin my own unofficial investigation. I was going to have to tackle the problem from another direction. Louisa had said something about two other girlfriends on Jerry's local route. That was certainly a road worth taking. Maybe the salesman had indeed been killed out of jealousy, but by a different girlfriend on his route.

At least I knew the other suspects, since I was focusing on Jerry's customers. I drove to nearby Sassafras Ridge and parked in front of The Soap Bubble, an upscale boutique that fought to be everything we weren't. The building had once been a residential cottage before Monique had converted it into a shop. The white picket fence in front was carefully weathered, and Monique's sign hanging from a verdigris standard looked as if it could have been a hundred years old. The cottage had ivy growing directly on the stone wall in front, and the door was painted a shocking shade of red that grabbed the attention of anyone walking past it.

It looked more like a Hollywood set than a soap shop. The ultimate truth was that the owner didn't believe in the intrinsic value of her product. To Monique White, soap was just a commodity, a widget to sell, whereas my Perkins clan had a love for soapmaking that was unquestioning. We had taken something that was a rather mundane household item to most folks and turned it into an art form. It was truly amazing how soap could be personalized using aromas, textures, colors, and shapes to cleanse, soothe, and rejuvenate the spirit as well as the body.

I'd run into the boutique owner a dozen times over the years. Monique was in her late thirties, though plastic surgery and a heavy application of cosmetics struggled to disguise the fact that she'd long ago left twenty-five behind. She had fine red hair, always coiffed in the latest style, and wore simple outfits that probably cost a fortune. She'd married well, and as she liked to say, divorced even better. The shop was a place for her to mingle with her friends and play at working. The store was deserted, most likely because her particular clientele probably hadn't crawled out of bed yet.

"Why if it isn't Ben Perkins, the Soap Master himself. What brings you here? Looking to copy my image and style?"

Hardly. "Your style is uniquely your own, Monique," I said, the truth of my intent eluding her.

"So it is. I'm still waiting for an answer, though. Why are you here?"

There was no easy way to do it, so I just blurted out, "I'm afraid I've come to deliver some bad news. Something's happened to one of our suppliers. Jerry Sanger is dead."

Monique looked at me as if I were joking, then she must have seen the severity in my face. "Ben, that's not funny."

"I'm not kidding, Monique."

She stared at me a few moments, then in a halting voice, she said, "He's really dead?"

"Murdered, actually."

"No, it can't be. He was supposed to come by the shop this afternoon. I can't believe it."

"It's true," I said. "How well did you know him?"

Softly crying, Monique buried her head in her hands for a full minute. I was beginning to suspect she'd forgotten I was there. Was she acting, or was this the first she was learning of Jerry Sanger's death? I honestly couldn't tell, though I considered myself a pretty good judge of character and the honesty of people's reactions. I'd never thought of Monique as particularly vulnerable, but maybe I hadn't given her a fair chance.

"Monique," I said softly, and that brought her back around.

Through her tears, she said, "I'm afraid I'm going to have to ask you to leave."

"You must have known him pretty well," I said, not budging. "I didn't think it would hit you this hard." Growing up in a large family had taught me to stand my ground when I needed anything, and at the moment, I needed an answer from Monique. I hated being a bully about it, but then I remembered where Louisa was, and my resolve firmed.

"He was one of my suppliers. We were friends, of a sort. That's all. Ben, why are you being so cold about this? A man we both knew is dead." She pushed me to the door, and as I stepped outside, I heard the dead bolt latch behind me. By the time I got back to my car, she had flipped the sign on the door from OPEN to CLOSED. It appeared that Jerry Sanger had been more than a supplier to Monique, no matter how much she'd protested. How much more than a friend, I still didn't know.

There was one more soap shop within driving distance I could check out, but I nearly didn't go. After all, the Kents were a kindly old couple married over forty years; I couldn't picture Amy Elizabeth Kent dallying with Jerry Sanger under any circumstances. But I'd been wrong before.

The Kents' shop in Hunter's Hollow was more to my liking, filled with scents and sights that did my heart good. Their storefront could barely be called that, a small nook among several other businesses that had gone through many incarnations before A Long Lost Soap had come into being. While our shelves were laid out in precise order, the aisles of this soap shop looked as if they'd been stocked randomly and without any sense of unity. The place would have given my mother a stroke, but it suited the Kents' personality.

There was someone new behind the counter when I walked in, an attractive blonde in her early twenties. "May I help you?"

"Are the Kents around?" I asked.

"They're on an extended cruise, but I'd be happy to help you. I'm most knowledgeable."

So that explained their absence. "I'm an old friend. My name's Ben Perkins. I work at Where There's Soap."

"Mr. Perkins, it's nice to meet you. I'm their granddaughter Heather. I've been running the shop for them for the past two weeks."

"That was nice of you," I said. "They must trust you a great deal."

When she smiled, her nose crinkled. "I believe they would have let someone off the street watch the place, they were so eager to go. However, I've been working here part-time since I transferred to Hopkins-Upshire." Hopkins-Upshire College—Hop Up U as the townsfolk called it—was the closest thing we had to a center for higher learning in our part of the state.

"You don't by any chance know Jerry Sanger, do you?"

I couldn't believe it when Heather blushed at the question. "Actually, we've been dating off and on for several weeks now. Why, has he been talking about me?"

"I don't know how to tell you this, but he's been murdered."

Heather nearly collapsed in tears as she heard the news. I was certainly a popular fellow today. There had to be a better way to tell people what had happened to Jerry Sanger, but I didn't have a clue how to do it. On the other hand, my method did get instant results.

As she cried, I asked her softly, "Heather, can I get you anything?"

She shook her head and looked up at me through red eyes. "No, I'll be fine. I just need to catch my breath. What happened to him?"

"Somebody pushed him down a flight of stairs." I didn't have the heart to add that they'd doused him in lye as well.

"How horrid." She slumped down into a chair. "I've never known anyone who's been murdered. Have they caught the person who did it yet?"

"The police are just starting to look at suspects. They may come by and talk to you sometime in the next few days."

It was amazing to watch her reaction to that statement. After a moment, Heather calmly said, "I don't know what I would have to tell them. Jerry and I went out a few times. It wasn't anything all that serious, just a casual relationship." She was backpedaling away from the earlier dating scenario so fast that by the time Molly caught up with her, I was certain Heather would be describing their relationship as distant but cordial.

A customer came in before I could ask Heather anything else. "Should I wait on them for you?" I asked. "I know my way around soap, and you look like you could use a minute."

She arched an eyebrow to the sky. "No, I'm fine. It was just a shock, hearing you blurt it out like that. Thank you for stopping by, Mr. Perkins. I'll tell my aunt and uncle you visited the next time they call."

There was no way I was letting myself be shuffled off that easily. "I'd like to discuss this a little further with you, if you don't mind. I'm not in any hurry, I can wait until you finish here."

"I'm afraid I don't know anything else," she said, dismissing me as she moved past and greeted her customer. "May I help you?"

Heather and the visitor were studying scents together as I left. So far my investigation had led to a big fat zero. I'd visited the two stores I was familiar with on the salesman's route, and I couldn't exactly barge into places where I wasn't known and start blurting out the news that Sanger was dead. All I'd managed so far was killing some gasoline and my morning. It was time to head back to Where There's Soap and see what had transpired in my absence. As I drove back to Harper's Landing, I couldn't help wondering if either woman had been totally forthright with me about her relationship with the route salesman. Both Monique and Heather had been more rattled by the news of Jerry Sanger's death than I'd expected, but did that make either one of them the killer? I wouldn't go that far without more evidence, but I did have to wonder if there had been more to both relationships than either woman had been willing to admit.

But were their overt reactions because of their dalliances, or were they inspired by guilty consciences?

WHEN I got back to the shop, Mom cornered me at the door before I could take my jacket off. "So, what did you find out?"

"Give me some time, Mom. I can't do this in a few hours—you should realize that."

She clucked a couple of times. "Benjamin, if you aren't finished, then why are you here?"

"I've got a class," I said, and before she could say anything herself, I added, "I'm teaching it, so don't try to convince me otherwise." I looked around the shop and saw that Cindy and Kate were waiting on customers. "Any word from Kelly yet?" I wondered how long Molly would grill my sister.

Mom said, "No, she didn't have much to say when she dropped Louisa off here half an hour ago."

"Louisa's here?" I asked, looking around.

Mom nodded. "She's in the break room. You should go talk to her, Benjamin."

"That sounds like a good idea," I said as I brushed past my mother. I could have used the information of my sister's return when it had happened instead of finding out so casually later. That was one of the reasons I had a cell phone—to keep in touch when I was away—but my mother hated to call me on it, afraid of running up my charges, no matter how much I tried to tell her otherwise.

I found Louisa sitting by herself in the break room, a forgotten cookie lying on a napkin in her lap.

"Wow, that was quick," I said as I walked in.

She nodded. "Kelly came in with guns blazing. Molly barely had a chance to ask me anything."

I noticed Louisa had on a different outfit. "Did Molly take your clothes?"

"I talked to Kelly about it, and since I've never worked with liquid lye, she told me it would be okay to surrender my outfit. Cindy brought me different clothes, even shoes. They didn't find lye on anything I had on, so I guess that's something."

"Come on, Louisa, that's great news."

"I got the feeling Molly thought I might have already changed before you found Jerry. Kelly said she'd probably get a warrant to go through my laundry."

"Well, you're free now, that's what counts."

Louisa asked softly, "Ben, you didn't have anything to do with this, did you? I know how protective you are of me. It's okay if you did, I won't judge you, I swear it."

It had been quite a day so far. My mother and sister had both asked me if I'd committed murder before breakfast. "Come on, you've got to be kidding. I might have whipped his fanny if I'd found out what he'd been doing to you, but I wouldn't have done this. Somebody wasn't satisfied with just killing him; that lye was a mark of revenge."

Louisa shivered, and I regretted my choice of words. I asked, "So where do things stand now with the police?"

"Molly said it was too soon to say when we'd talk again, especially with Kelly's constant interruptions, but she told me she wasn't done with me yet."

I put a hand on my sister's shoulder. "It's going to be all right. Listen, why don't you stay with Cindy or Kate until this thing blows over? Heck, for that matter you could come bunk with me."

She shook her head. "The last thing anybody in the family needs is me underfoot. Besides, I like living alone. Don't worry, I'll be fine."

"Well, if you change your mind, you can always have my couch."

"I'd have to be pretty desperate to sleep there," she said.

I tried to ease her rightfully heavy mood. "Okay, okay, you can have the bed and I'll take the sofa. Just know that you're welcome any time."

She patted my cheek. "I know. Thanks, Ben. What would I do without my big brother?"

I smiled. "Let's hope you never have to find out." I glanced at the clock, then said, "I've lost all track of time. I have a melt-and-pour beginner's class I'm teaching in twenty minutes and I haven't even had lunch yet."

Louisa gestured toward the goodies table piled high behind us. "Help yourself."

Promising myself an extra two-mile walk that night, I grabbed a plate and chose the smallest piece of apple pie I could find. It was still enough to make a meal when I added a glass of milk from the refrigerator.

THE classroom was nearly full as I entered our teaching area, a walled-off room that contained five long tables covered with the basic equipment we'd be using over the next four afternoons. There were nine people there out of the ten registered; it was proof that soapmaking was indeed becoming a quite popular hobby. An older woman sitting with her husband at one of the front tables told me, "We're so excited to be here. Your class is a gift from our grandchildren."

"Well, at least one of us is thrilled," the man said quietly. "No offense, but I'd rather be fishing."

She poked him in the ribs. "Herbert Wilson, you're here, and what's more, you're going to have fun."

"Well, I'm here, Constance. I'll admit to that much."

I could tell Herbert was going to be a handful, but I didn't mind skeptics attending my classes. Sometimes they added a much needed leavening to the earnestness of my normal students.

I addressed the class. "Ladies," and with a wink at Herbert, "and gentlemen, welcome to the world of soapmaking. I hope you all will enjoy this class, and that it won't be a wash for any of you." There were several chuckles, but none from Herbert. "Soap, in one form or another, has been with us since the dawn of Man. There are records of soapmaking as far back as 2500 B.C., and legends and myths were created to explain its discovery. In short, making soap is a bit like re-creating history.

"Now, why don't we get started? In front of you, you'll find every tool you'll need to produce the most elegant of soaps. Not very high-tech, is it? In fact, most of the equipment you'll ever need is already in your kitchen." As I mentioned the tools we'd be using, I held them up and named them. "We've got glass mixing bowls, thermometers, measuring bowls, cups, and spoons; there are hand graters, wooden spoons, drying racks, and sharp knives. Then there's the safety equipment, like these plastic gloves, goggles, and smocks."

Herbert mumbled, "It sounds more like a chemistry class than one on soapmaking."

I applauded, then asked Herbert to say it again louder. He did so, albeit reluctantly, and I added, "Class, that is exactly what we're doing. I'm sure you all know that cooking requires a great deal of chemistry: weighing, measuring, mixing, and heating to the correct temperature. Many of you are already pros at these things, so you've got a natural advantage in soapmaking."

A hand went up at one of the tables, and an elderly woman with blue-tinted hair asked timidly, "Will we be working with lye? My grandmother was burned something awful when I was a little girl, and she had the scars until the day she died."

I could see the fear in her eyes, and I did my best to ease her concern. "Let me assure you, you all will be perfectly safe. This course is going to cover the process of one of the two basic techniques for soapmaking that don't require lye: the melt-and-pour method. The other type, hand-milling, is taught in a different class. The other two processes, aptly named cold and hot, require the active use of lye. For melt-and-pour—that's what we'll be tackling this week—we'll be using a basic soap foundation, melting it and then enhancing it. For the hand-milling process, you begin with a basic bar of white soap with no color or fragrance added, and then amend it."

The woman frowned at my reply. "I thought we'd be making our own soap from scratch."

"We do that here in our production area in back, and there's another class that covers those basics as well. For this class, we start with a transparent soap medium, and we employ it just like any other basic material like the oils and scents we use. Believe me, after you finish individualizing your soaps, they will genuinely be unique, handcrafted products." It was a sticking point for some crafters who insisted on doing everything from scratch. I couldn't see their point. After all, no one expected them to grow their own herbs, though we did just that in our production garden out front. The essential oils we used were already processed somewhat. The basic form of the soap itself was no different, in my opinion.

One of the women asked, "So how exactly do we make them so unique? Is there a formula or something we follow?"

"I like to think of it more as a recipe, myself. What you add to your soap depends on how you plan to use it. Let's say you're interested in creating a soap that helps the user relax. You might choose to add lavender, clary sage, chamomile, tangerine, rose, or lemon verbena. Or, if you wanted something more energizing, you might choose rosemary, peppermint, lemon, lime, or jasmine."

"What if you wanted something for insomnia?" Herbert asked softly. A split second later, his wife poked him in the ribs, but I took it as a serious question. I told the class, "Herbert wants a cure for insomnia. Chamomile's good for that, and so are orange and lavender." I let my gaze sweep through the room as I continued, "But we don't have to stop there. We can add abrasives like luffa sponge or ground almonds to the mix, antioxidants such as fruits and vegetables, emollients like glycerine and almond oil, refrigerants like mint, and let's not forget colorants. Nearly whatever soap you can imagine, you can make. Now who's ready to get started?"

Every hand went up, though Herbert's required a solid poke from his wife first. I smiled broadly at them, then said, "Then let's get down to business, shall we?"

As everyone surveyed the ingredients in front of them, there were laughs and the buzz of happy conversation. It was why I loved giving the classes, sharing a lifetime of knowledge and experience with folks so eager to learn.

I was about to start teaching the actual process when the back door of the classroom opened.

My brother Jeff rushed in, and from the expression on his face, I knew there was more trouble with the Perkins clan before he even had a chance to open his mouth.

THREE

○ ○ ○

"EXCUSE me for one second," I told my students as I walked back to Jeff.

"What is it?" I asked quietly when I got to the door. We had a rule in our family that when someone was teaching a class, they weren't to be interrupted unless the building was on fire.

I could tell from his expression that my brother could feel the sting in my words. "It's Molly. She's coming over in half an hour to talk to you."

"Did she say what it was about?"

He shook his head. "No, that's what's got us all concerned. Ben, Mom wants you to cancel your class right now. Everybody else who could take over for you is busy right now."

I couldn't believe what I was hearing. I had realized my mother was shook up by the murder, as she had every right to be, but I'd never known her to give a refund in her life, and someone would have every right to demand one if we just threw them out. "Jeff, there's nothing I can do until Molly gets here. Class should be over by then. If she shows up early, come get me."

"Mom's not going to like it," Jeff said.

"She'll just have to get over it."

I walked back to the front of the class, wondering what Molly had on her mind. Mom was rattled even more than she'd shown if she was willing to cancel one of our soap-making classes, and it wasn't just about the money. Offering lessons was her way of proselytizing to the world, and the sessions we held in our shop were almost sacrosanct.

"Sorry for the interruption," I told the class. "Now let's make some soap."

I held up a chunk of the transparent base and said, "For this process, all you need is a glass microwavable dish, a mold, and some hot water."

Herbert said, "That's not soapmaking, that's melting." I knew he didn't realize I could hear him, but the man's hearing must have been going; all of his comments were audible enough to me in front of the class.

"Some of you might think it's too simplistic." I grinned at Herbert, and he looked at me like he thought I was reading his mind. I continued, "What makes it your unique soap is what you include while the base is in its liquid form. You can add dyes and scents; you can even imbed objects in your soap." I showed them some examples I'd made just for that class, including one that sported a seashell and another with a plastic frog. "We have four microwaves, so you'll have to share. Each of you needs to get eight small cubes of the base—we've already cut them up for you today—then slice off some of the soap color and add it to the bowl if you'd like your soap tinted. Give it a thirty-second burst at full power, check to see if it's melted, then nuke it five seconds at a time until it's liquid. Select your additives—remember, a little goes a long way—then stir them into the mix and pour the liquid into the molds you've selected. It's as easy as that." I strolled around the room, working with the class as they made their first soaps. Even Herbert seemed to be pleased with his rather mundane choice of a blue square of unscented soap. "No fragrance?" I asked, smelling the blend.

"No, I wanted to try something easy the first time. It looks okay, doesn't it?"

I patted him on the back. "It looks great."

"Can I take it out of the mold now?"

"No, I forgot to mention that, didn't I?" I spoke up to the class as they worked. "Your creations will take about an hour to set up. Feel free to make more. We have lots of molds to choose from, and there's plenty of materials." Truthfully, I didn't care how many soaps they made. They were paying for the privilege with their class fees, and besides, that was why we offered only four microwaves. Melting the soap took time, and it was the one part of the process that couldn't be rushed.

As the clock kept ticking closer to the end of class, I kept glancing back at the door. I had been right not to cancel the class, but I still couldn't help wondering what was so urgent about Molly's visit.

I waited until the second hand made its final sweep, then told the class, "That wraps up today's session. You're welcome to look around the shop while you wait for your creations to harden. If you don't want to stay, I'll be glad to take your soaps out of their molds and wrap them for you as soon as they set. That way you can pick up your handiwork tomorrow afternoon during our next class." There were good reasons to offer them the choice; if they stayed around, most of the class members would probably browse around in the boutique and buy things in our shop. If they didn't, having a handmade soap waiting for them next time brought them back to our place. It was a win-win situation for Where There's Soap, a clever twist Mom had put in herself.

As I sent my students out into the shop, I started cleaning up the mess that was always left behind after a soap-making session. I was just finishing up when Molly came in, an agitated expression on her face that spelled trouble for me.

"SINCE when did you start butting into my business?" Molly demanded without saying hello.

Ordinarily I wouldn't stand for that tone of voice from her, but I knew she had every reason in the world to be upset with me if she had any idea what I was up to. I just wasn't sure how much she knew at this point. I offered her my best grin. "That depends. How long have you known me?"

I didn't even get the ghost of a smile in response, so I knew she was really angry. "Save your charm for someone else, Ben; this is serious. You had no right going to those two shops ahead of me. I could lock you up for obstruction of justice."

"Why, just because I visited some of my competitors today?"

She frowned. "No, for tipping my hand and telling both women about Sanger before I could. When I interview people, I'm interested in more than what they say. I study body language, mannerisms, tone of voice. I'm trained to do this, and you're not. Ben, this behavior is completely unacceptable. How am I supposed to run an investigation with you mucking things up playing amateur detective?"

Okay, she had a point. "I'm sorry," I said. "Mom was upset, and she wanted me to talk to a few people in the business. Come on, you know what a force she can be when she puts her mind to it."

"You can't go digging into this case. I mean it."

I held my wrists out to her. "You're right, but there's only one way you can be sure of stopping me. You'd better go ahead and lock me up."

She rolled her eyes, a sight I was long used to. "Spare me the dramatics." Molly frowned a second, then asked, "So how did they react when you told them Sanger was dead?"

I shared my observations with her, then I added, "You know, you might be able to use me on this."

She barely acknowledged my offer with a glance. "How do you figure that?"

"Molly, you're a great cop, but you don't know anything about the soapmaking world. I know the processes, and more importantly, I know the people. They might open up to me when they'd never dream of telling you anything. This happened in my world."

"Ben, I appreciate the offer, but I'm doing fine on my own." She flipped her wallet open. "See? I have a badge and everything."

She wasn't going to be mollified, but Molly was smart. If I gave her some time to get used to the idea, I might even get her blessing for my snooping. I couldn't stop, not with Louisa in her sights, but it would make my life a whole lot easier if Molly accepted my input. I asked, "Is that the only reason you came out here?"

She nodded. "It's reason enough. I was so mad at you I could have spit nails. I'll talk to you later."

"I'll be counting the minutes," I said, grinning as I tweaked her arm.

After she was gone, Mom cornered me in the classroom. "Did she come to arrest your sister?"

"No, Ma'am, that visit was strictly about me. Molly wanted to read me the riot act for talking to her suspects. She was not at all pleased."

"That's wonderful," Mom said, beaming.

That was entirely a matter of opinion. "What's so great about that? I got chewed out pretty hard."

"Don't you see? She's willing to consider someone else besides your sister. Keep digging, Benjamin. You always did have a knack for stirring up trouble."

"Hey, we all have to be good at something."

As my students wandered among the soapmaking supplies and designer soaps, I wondered how much more stirring I'd get away with before Molly actually decided to lock me up after all.

"YOU had a phone call," my sister Kate told me as I walked past the checkout counter.

She handed me a sheet from the yellow pad we used for messages, but the only thing on it was Monique White's name, The Soap Bubble's number, and a brief note that said "Call me." "What did she want?" I asked.

Kate said, "She wouldn't say. There was something odd about her voice, though."

"Anything you could put your finger on?" My sister was as good a judge of character as anyone I'd ever known, and she'd been the only one in the family besides me who had scorned Jerry Sanger's romantic pursuit of our sister. That alone should have told Louisa that she was making a mistake, but the heart wants what the heart wants.

Kate scrunched her lips together, something she'd done since childhood when she was searching for the right word. "She'd been crying, that was easy enough to tell, but there was more to it than that. Ben, she sounded, I don't know, kind of lost."

"I'd better call her back right away," I said.

Kate looked steadily at me, then asked, "You haven't been going out with our competition on the sly, have you, Big Brother?"

"Like I could ever keep anything from this family," I said.

"You never know. You can be sneaky when you want to be," Kate said.

I shook my head. "I'm sorry to report that my love life has been a bit stark lately."

Kate said, "You know who you should ask out? Kelly Sheer. She's perfect for you."

I looked at my sister like she'd lost her mind. "You've got to be kidding. After the divorce she just went through, I'm sure she's sworn off men for the rest of her life."

Kate shook her head, then spoke in a condescending manner that the Perkins women had fully mastered when dealing with men. "Come on, don't be dense, Ben. I've seen the way she looks at you when you're not watching. Do you honestly think it's your vast soapmaking skills she's so interested in?"

"I don't know," I said. "To be honest with you, I never really noticed."

She sighed. "It's a wonder you men ever do. So are you going to ask her out, or are you content living your cold and joyless little life alone until the day you die?"

"Sis, just because you're overcome with wedded bliss doesn't mean everyone's searching for their soul mate."

"Don't kid yourself, Ben, people weren't meant to be alone."

I gestured around at my brothers and sisters. "How could I ever be alone with all of you? Sometimes I have to step outside to have a thought without someone else reading my mind. Besides, I'm not alone. There's always Molly."

Kate wasn't buying that. "Regardless of what Mom says, if you two were going to get together, it would have happened by now. You and Molly are just using each other as crutches, and it's not healthy for either one of you. You can't play it safe for the rest of your life, Ben."

"Thanks for the lecture," I said. "Kate, I know you mean well, but my love life really isn't any of your business."

This particular sister had never been affected by bluntness. She smiled, then said, "First you need a love life before I can snoop into it. Think about what I said."

"Oh, I will," I said as insincerely as I could manage.

I went upstairs to the loft where our offices were, thinking about what Kate had said despite my reply to her. Certainly Kelly Sheer was an attractive woman, and I loved the way she had thrown herself into soapmaking. She had a nice smile, too, but that didn't mean she was interested in me, no matter what my delusional sister believed. I brushed it out of my thoughts as I dialed Monique's number.

It rang seven times before her answering machine kicked in. I gave her my home number on the machine, told her I was sorry I'd missed her, and stuffed the note in my pocket. Was Monique calling to confess, or was there some less ominous reason for her message? I'd have to try her again later.

I looked through the paperwork on my desk, but there was nothing pressing that needed my immediate attention. Mom and I were the only ones with offices upstairs, since Grandpa had given his up years before. Whenever he did decide to come in and work, he set up shop wherever was most convenient for him, and that rarely meant his designated space. Since our offices were just over the production line, glass windows looked down on the storefront below, and I could see Herbert and his wife milling about, loaded down with enough supplies to clean our part of North Carolina. I glanced at the clock and saw that it was time to go back downstairs and finish up with the projects from my class. Their soaps would be set by now, and I knew my pupils still there were eager to take home their first efforts at soapmaking.

The sales floor was crowded, so I approached my

students individually and soon had them all back to the classroom. As I showed them how to pop their soaps out of the molds by pushing from the bottom and twisting, they laughed and chatted happily, doing it themselves. "Let's wrap these up and you'll be ready to check out," I said. Several of the shopping baskets were laden with supplies and soaps. It looked like another successful attempt at recruiting new soapmakers. After their soaps were wrapped, I said, "Thanks for coming. I'll see you all tomorrow at our next class."

Herbert and his wife Constance hesitated at the classroom door. She nudged him once before Herbert would say, "Thanks for the class."

"So, do you mind if I ask how you liked it?" I asked, fighting my grin.

"It was pretty good, actually." He smiled slightly, then added, "This wasn't nearly as big a waste of time as I thought it was going to be." He deftly stepped aside as his wife's elbow lashed out for his gut. "I'm kidding," Herbert explained to her. "He knows that."

I laughed. "See you both tomorrow afternoon."

His wife Constance was still scolding him as they approached the register.

I saw Louisa pitching in at the checkout line, bagging purchases as quickly as Cindy could ring them up, but I could tell my eldest sister wanted to be a million miles away. I grabbed Kate from the sales floor and asked, "Why don't you give Louisa a break? I want to talk to her for a minute."

Kate nodded, and in a minute Louisa joined me. As she approached, she said, "Kate said you wanted to talk to me."

"Let's take a walk," I said.

Louisa looked around the boutique, then said, "There are too many customers here right now. They need me, Ben."

"Kate and Cindy have it under control," I said as I took

her arm. "Besides, Mom can pitch in if they need an extra hand. Most of that line is from my class, and they're on their way out. Come on, we can check out the garden and talk a little."

I knew the herb garden in front of the shop where we raised some of our additives was one of Louisa's favorite places in the world. A bench sat in the center of the herbs, with a small waterfall trickling under the shaded arbor. Though we were close to the road, the splashing water drowned out most of the sounds from the street. It was like taking a vacation with only twenty steps, and I'd found the retreat a great place to get away myself. Roses and scented geraniums bordered the plot, giving the whole area a floral edging. As we strolled through the rows of chamomile, lavender, verbena, mint, and sage, I asked Louisa, "How are you holding up?"

"Do you want to know the truth? I'm in shock. If this had happened yesterday, I would have been upstairs crying for weeks. As it is, I'm not sure what I feel. It's strange, wishing someone ill and then finding it happen almost immediately, like I had some kind of macabre power."

"I'm still your favorite brother, right?" I asked with a smile. "No bad feelings shooting my way?" Ordinarily my comment would have been in extremely poor taste, but then I didn't have the same relationship with anyone else in the world that I had with this particular sister.

Louisa said, "You don't have to worry about me, I'll think good thoughts about you." Her slight smile vanished as she added, "That phone call this morning rattled me more than I'm willing to admit. It's been bothering me nearly as much as seeing Jerry lying there on our steps. That woman was vicious when she called."

"And you're sure you didn't recognize the voice?" I asked.

Louisa said, "It was kind of familiar, but it was almost

like she was disguising it, you know? I keep thinking it will come to me, but I can't put my finger on it, at least not yet. Give me time, though, I'll figure it out."

That opened another worry I hadn't considered up to that point. "Have you ever thought you might be in danger?" I asked.

"Why do you say that? I didn't kill Jerry. I swear it."

I shook my head. "Sis, I know you didn't, but whoever did could have been the woman who called you. Otherwise it's too big a coincidence to believe it happened just before Jerry died, and I'm not a big fan of happenstance."

"So why does that put me in danger?"

"Think about it. She called you and spilled Jerry's secret, then got mad all over again and tracked him down here. After she killed him, she decided to cover her tracks, and she had to know you might be able to identify her voice. Sis, I hate to say this, but you shouldn't be alone until this thing is over."

"I'm not running and hiding, Ben; I won't do it. I think your imagination is working overtime."

"So humor me," I said as we sat on the bench. "Stay with somebody, even if it's Bob."

"I'd rather stay with you," she said. After a few moments of thought, she said, "You know, I could always bunk with Kate. She's been after me to try out her new guest room for months. She's so proud of her decorating skills." Louisa studied me a second, then said, "The only reason I'm doing this is because I know that if I don't, you'll drag Mom into this."

"Me?" I said, trying my best to look innocent.

"You." She kept her gaze on the patch of chamomile. "Listen, I didn't have a chance to say anything to you before, but I appreciate you looking into this mess for me. It makes me feel better knowing you're snooping around behind the scenes."

I put my arm around her. "Molly's not too thrilled about it, but I can't just stand by and let you get steamrolled into a murder charge you don't merit."

Her smile was brief, but it was full and bright. "Thanks, Ben, I appreciate you looking out for me. It's like third grade all over again, isn't it?"

I loved seeing my sister's smile, if only for a second or two. "I wish I could make this go away as easily as I scared Calvin Evans. He shouldn't have picked on you."

"After you talked to him, he never did again." She took my hands in hers and said in a deadly serious tone of voice, "Ben, make this go away. I really need you."

"I'm doing my best," I said. "Listen, I hate to bring this up, but I need to know more about Jerry Sanger if I'm going to figure out what happened to him. Would it hurt too much to tell me a little about him?"

"I don't know how much help I can be, but what did you want to know?" Louisa asked quietly.

"It might help if I knew where he lived, places he liked to hang out, his friends, his enemies if you know them; anything you can tell me might make a real difference."

"I'm embarrassed to say that I didn't know that much about his life. I was at his apartment downtown a few times. It was almost as if nobody really lived there, you know?"

"Do you mean there were boxes and things sitting all around?" I asked. "Some people take forever to unpack."

"No, I mean nothing was there. He had a bed, a kitchen table, and two chairs. That was about it."

"Did you ever ask him about it?"

She stared at the fountain a minute, then said, "He claimed he spent so much time on the road it didn't make any sense to have a nice place, but I got the feeling he was hiding something."

That might be worth looking into. Was it possible that

Jerry had rented the place he'd taken Louisa as a dodge? Was he hiding something from her, like maybe a wife somewhere else on his route? Molly would know, but I didn't have a clue how I could ask her. I said, "Is there anything else you can think of that might help?"

"I know he liked to hang out at Dying to Read—we went there a few times together—but that's about it. Jerry didn't like to eat out, and I ended up cooking for him in his apartment most of the times we went out. He really had me going. I'm sorry, Ben."

Jerry Sanger sounded like a real prince all the way around. At least Louisa had told me one thing that I could follow up on myself. Dying to Read was a mystery bookstore that had recently opened in Harper's Landing. In the six months since they'd been in business, I'd visited the shop three or four times. I've got a weakness for mysteries, but I'd never run into Jerry Sanger there. I was sure Molly had his apartment covered—what little there was to see there, anyway. That left the bookstore for me.

"Listen," I said as I stood. "I'll do what I can, but don't let this get you down if you can help it. Louisa, we both know you didn't do anything wrong."

"Nothing criminal, anyway. I should have used better judgment choosing my dates. Next time I'm going to listen to Kate."

I knew Louisa was feeling low if she was willing to admit that. "Hey, nobody's going to arrest you for being human. Are you going to be all right?"

"I'll manage. Where are you off to?"

"I'm going to go look for a good book," I said, hoping I could turn up some kind of clue at the mystery bookstore about what had really happened to Jerry Sanger on the steps of my shop.

FOUR

∘ ∘ ∘

IT was wonderful having a small, independent mystery bookstore like Dying to Read in our town. As I walked inside the cozy space, I could smell the coffee even before I could shut the thick oak door behind me. I surveyed the overstuffed couches spread amongst the wooden cherry shelves as soft music played in the background. Embedded in the hardwood floor mosaic at the entrance was the outline of a body, done in dark red mahogany inlaid in a field of white oak planking.

"Hi, welcome back," the clerk said, a college-aged young man with a full beard and jet-black hair pulled back into a ponytail. His badge said his name was Rufus, and it sported vivid drops of what I was certain were meant to be red blood below his name. The IDs were new, and catching to the eye.

"Thanks," I said as I looked around the crowded room.

The place was doing very well for itself, if the attendance at the moment was any indication.

"Something I can help you with?" he asked.

As I approached his position behind the cash register, I said, "I'm looking for the manager or the owner."

He smiled. "They're both the same lady. Hang on a second." He picked up the phone and said, "Diana, there's someone up front to see you."

He put the phone down and said, "She'll be out in a second."

I moved away from the desk as Rufus waited on a few customers. I looked over the display table where that month's best sellers were stacked and glanced at some of the covers. I was studying the crazy image of a lighthouse in the middle of a mountain range when someone said, "Excuse me, but were you looking for me?"

The owner was a tall, solid woman, matching my six-foot height exactly. Her long brown hair was pulled away from her face, and she appeared to be somewhere in her early thirties. She had big brown eyes, just like a deer's, and one of the noblest noses I'd ever seen on a man or a woman.

I offered my hand, and she took it in her steady grip for a moment before releasing it. "Hi, my name's Ben Perkins. I need to ask you about one of your customers."

"I'm Diana. May I ask what this is about?"

Here we go again, I thought to myself. I took a deep breath, then said, "A man named Jerry Sanger was murdered today, and my sister is one of the police's main suspects. I'm hoping you'll be able to help me prove she didn't do it." I still didn't like the way it sounded—announcing Sanger's demise like that—and I'd echoed the words enough lately to last me a lifetime.

She touched my arm as she lowered her voice in a

conspiratorial fashion. "Why don't we go back to my office? We'll have some privacy there."

I followed her through a door marked STAFF ONLY and found a tight office jammed with enough paperwork and books to drive me crazy if I had to face it every day.

Diana said apologetically, "Excuse the mess." Then a smile appeared briefly. "I don't know why I always say that; this place is constantly a wreck. It's an occupational hazard. Believe it or not, I can lay my hands on just about anything I need to with things organized this way."

As she moved a stack of books from her visitor's chair, I said, "I'm sorry to bother you, but I don't know where else to look."

"Honestly, it's no trouble at all." As I sat down, she said, "You know, I'd almost forgotten the color of the material on this chair. There, that's better. We can talk in here. Now what's this about a murder?"

"First off, I want you to know that you're not under any kind of obligation or anything to talk to me, but I honestly could use your help."

Diana said, "I'll do what I can, believe me. Ben, I wouldn't have opened a mystery bookstore if I didn't enjoy my share of amateur sleuthing."

"Diana, with all respect, this is real life. I found the body myself, and it wasn't a pretty sight."

She nodded. "Of course, you're right. It's just sometimes you get so inured to bodies in my line of work, when it really happens, it loses some of its edge. Do you have a picture of this Sanger? His name doesn't ring any bells."

I'd gotten the only photo Louisa had of Jerry. She had squirmed a little as I'd folded it in half lengthwise, but I wasn't about to parade a photograph of my sister across town beside a dead man if I could help it. I'd wanted to cut her out of the shot completely, but she'd thrown such a fit I'd decided to just fold it instead. It was a shot of the two of them taken candidly outside. I recognized my sister Cindy's ambush style of picture taking without needing confirmation. Louisa had told me that Jerry had been camera shy, and that she'd asked Cindy to snap something when he wasn't looking. I had to admit, given the reluctance of the subject, she'd done a good job in capturing him.

Diana studied the photo, then nodded. "I feel sorry for your sister if she was seeing him."

"Why's that?" I asked as I retrieved the snapshot.

"He hit on anything in a skirt here. I'm not sure why he chose this place—maybe he liked mysteries a little—but he was here more for my female clientele than anything in print. What happened to him?"

"My guess is that he died from a broken neck, and then someone gave him a bath in lye," I said.

"It sounds like something a jealous woman would do." She shivered. "And you found him. How terrible that must have been for you."

"Let's just say it's not something I'll forget any time soon. Was there anybody in particular he talked to while he was here?"

She shook her head. "Not that I could tell, but then again, I spend more time buried back here than I do in front waiting on customers. Why don't we ask Rufus?"

I followed her out of her office and we approached the front desk. Rufus was doing a crossword puzzle now that his line was gone, and he didn't look the least bit embarrassed at being caught goofing off on the job. Diana told me, "Show him the photo, Ben."

I did so, refolding the edge so most of Louisa's face was obscured. Rufus said, "Yeah, I know him. That's the shark."

"The shark?"

Rufus just shrugged. "That's my little nickname for him. He moved in for the kill faster than anybody I've ever seen before. It was like the dude was trying to prove he could do it, you know what I mean?"

Diana asked, "Was there anyone in particular he liked to talk with?"

Rufus was suddenly curious about our interrogation. "Why, what's he done?"

"He was murdered," Diana said simply. At least I hadn't been the one who had to break the news this time.

"Cool," Rufus replied, then looked sheepish about his response. "Sorry, I just never met anyone before who was murdered. What happened to him, did a jealous husband off him?"

Diana said, "We'll talk about the details later. Think, Rufus. Did you see him with anyone in particular?"

Rufus shook his head. "Nope, not that I can remember."

"Come on," Diana said, "this is important."

"There was one woman," Rufus finally admitted. "He wasn't at all happy to see her here, and they had quite a row."

"Do you know her name?" I asked.

Rufus shrugged, then idly opened the photograph and stared at Louisa. "You've got a picture of her right there. They were arguing in the hard-boiled section last week. I had to ask them to quiet down or leave. It wasn't pretty."

That was a detail my sister had neglected to mention. I wondered what else she hadn't told me. I asked, "Was there anybody else? Anybody at all?"

Rufus said, "No, sorry I can't help. He never seemed to hit on the same woman twice, whether he was successful with them or not. It was like somebody was keeping score, you know?"

"That's fine," I said. "I appreciate your help."

Diana walked me to the door. "Ben, if there's anything I can do, just let me know."

"I will," I said as I headed out.

"Come back any time," she added with interest, but I

was in too much of a hurry to stay and chat, as appealing as the prospect would have been under normal circumstances. She was, after all, an attractive woman, and smart, too. There was no time to pursue anything with her, though. At the moment, I had a pressing need to find my sister Louisa. We were going to have to talk about what else she wasn't telling me. Louisa had had every opportunity to mention her public squabble with Jerry to me, but she hadn't breathed a word about it. As I drove to her apartment, I wondered if she'd wanted me to find out after all. Why else would she have mentioned the bookstore to me? It didn't make Louisa guilty in my mind, not of anything more than bad judgment in not sharing everything with me, but if I was going to be of any use to her at all, I had to convince her that she needed to tell me everything, no matter how trivial it might seem to her. Though it was looking worse and worse for her, I still couldn't see Louisa killing someone, even with justification. Halfway to her place, I remembered her promise to stay at Kate's that night. It was in the other direction, but I figured I might as well keep driving to her apartment. Knowing Louisa, she'd probably changed her mind about staying somewhere else anyway. She had a will of her own that had been getting her into trouble her entire life.

When I got there, I immediately knew I'd been right in driving to her place first; the lights were blazing away in her apartment.

I could tell by her lack of a response that Louisa wasn't in the mood for company, but I didn't care. She finally answered her door the third time I leaned on the buzzer.

"Ben, what are you doing here? I was just on my way to Kate's house. You don't have to watch over me like I'm some kind of child."

"Somebody's got to," I said. "Let's go inside. You and I need to talk."

She glanced at her watch. "Sorry, but I'm late as it is. Kate's expecting me, and you know how she worries."

"She's just going to have to live with it," I said. "This can't wait."

"What's so urgent?" Louisa asked as she moved out of the way so I could go into her apartment. My sister's taste in art and furniture usually made me nauseous, and this trip was no different. I liked earth tones and impressionist prints, whereas Louisa went for brash colors and abstracts that gave me migraines every time I walked in.

I tried to keep my eyes diverted from the cacophony of color as I said, "I need to know what else you've been keeping from me."

"I don't know what you're talking about."

How she managed to say that with a straight face, I'd never know. "Come on, Sis, why else would you steer me to Dying to Read? You wanted me to find out about your fight with Jerry. I'm betting you didn't say a word to Molly about it, either. What kind of game do you think you're playing?"

Louisa slumped down into a burgundy sky chair hanging from her ceiling. "I didn't kill him, Ben, you've got to believe me."

I wanted to feel bad for her, but she was driving me crazy. "Of course I do, you nit, but you're not making it any easier for me. What was the fight about?" Before she could answer, I shook my head and said, "Please, just don't tell me you already knew about his womanizing before that telephone call this morning."

Louisa studied her hands, refusing to meet my gaze, and I knew I'd hit home. I said, "You knew before the phone call this morning, didn't you?"

She tried to blow the question off, but I wouldn't let her. "Louisa, tell me the truth."

Finally, she said, "Okay, I'll admit that I had my

suspicions, but there wasn't any real proof, not until I got the call this morning. I swear it."

"Louisa, you need to call Kelly, and I mean right now. If you won't tell me everything, you should at least tell her before Molly finds out on her own. It's going to look ten times worse for you if you don't volunteer the information."

My sister snapped, "How is Molly going to know anything about it?"

I handed Louisa her telephone. "Come on, Molly's going to find out, and it's going to be sooner than later; she's good at what she does, and you didn't do all that great a job of hiding your argument. Half a dozen people probably overheard you two, and the second Jerry's picture hits the papers, somebody's bound to call the police."

Louisa looked genuinely concerned as she retrieved Kelly's business card and dialed the number on it. Good. She needed a good scare to get her to come clean.

After a few words, Louisa hung the telephone up. "She's coming right over. She was going to a movie, but Kelly said this was more important. Ben, can you stay here with me until she shows up? I'm getting scared."

"I don't know. I've got a thousand things I have to do." Honestly, there was nothing pressing, but I was still miffed at my sister for keeping something from me.

In a voice that reminded me of the child she'd been, Louisa said, "Please?"

I patted her arm. All of my hard feelings were washed away with her simple request. "Of course I'll stay. Tell you what, why don't we make some tea while we're waiting? Are you still drinking that English stuff?"

"I'm trying Eastern Bud blends now, but I've got Lipton for you, don't worry." I was pretty pedestrian in my tea tastes, while Louisa loved the different exotic blends she'd found on the Internet.

The tea was ready by the time the doorbell rang. Louisa

asked, "Go let her in, would you? I'll make up a tray for us."

I couldn't believe my sister. "This isn't a party—Kelly's here on business."

"Just get the door, Ben," she said.

I answered the summons and found Kelly Sheer standing there with a briefcase tucked under one arm. Her blonde hair was pulled back into a ponytail and she wore wire-rimmed glasses perched on her nose. Instead of the suit I half expected to see her wearing, Kelly had on an attractive green print dress that brought out the emerald shades of her eyes and showed off her shapely legs. She was pretty in a way that was hard to describe, and I wondered why more folks didn't think she was attractive. I'd heard her described as strong, even fierce when she was in court, and one of my customers had once called her a handsome woman, but I thought she was adorable, though I'd never tell her that.

"So that's what lawyers wear to the movies," I said as she walked in past me.

"I was dressed a little more appropriately for my plans this evening, but Louisa sounded desperate. Besides, I already had a sitter for Annie, so I was free."

"Thanks for canceling your date," I said. "You need to hear what Louisa's been up to."

Kelly explained, "It wasn't a date; just a few friends getting together for a show. What's going on?"

"I think you should hear it from my sister."

Louisa came into the living room with the tray. "Thanks for coming, Kelly. Would you like some tea?"

"Later, perhaps," she said as she put her briefcase down on the sofa. "Right now I'd like to hear this important news."

"I'll be going then," I said as I moved toward the door. "You two don't need me here."

Louisa said, "You can stay, Ben. Honestly, I don't mind."

"Sorry, but maybe it's a good idea if you do go, Ben," Kelly said. "I don't want anything to jeopardize the attorney–client privilege. Sorry."

"That's fine with me," I said. "I'll see you both later."

I left them alone and headed home. There was nowhere I needed to be until morning, and I was worn-out from running all over my part of North Carolina looking for clues. My toe-dip into investigating had given me a lot more respect for Molly and what she did than I ever had before. I'd talked to five people so far, and at least three of them had lied to me, including my own sister. Digging into Jerry Sanger's life was going to be a lot more difficult than I'd thought, but I didn't have much choice. Even if I was willing to let it go, Mom wasn't about to ease up on me until someone else was charged with Sanger's murder. If I had to choose between nosing into the dead man's life or getting grief from my mother, it was an easy decision; I'd rather track down a killer than face my mom's nagging.

As I drove to my apartment, sudden fat raindrops started pounding down on my windshield and the ragtop of my Miata. It leaked around the edges—I'd never owned a convertible that didn't—and by the time I arrived at my apartment, the humidity inside the car was nearly 100 percent. I owned a perfectly good umbrella. The only problem was that it was two hundred yards away, hanging in my closet. I grabbed the morning newspaper from the floor and tried to shield myself from the brunt of the downpour as I ran for my door, but I was still pretty wet by the time I slipped inside my apartment.

I was drying my hair with a towel when I noticed that there was a message on my machine. It was Monique, and from the sound of her voice, I was willing to bet she'd been drinking most of the evening. "Ben, where are you? Call me, you've got my number. Bye."

I dialed her number, let it ring a dozen times, then killed

the connection. Was she sleeping, or had she gone out? Passed out, most likely. I hit redial and tried again, resolved to keep trying until morning if I had to. That's when I realized that her machine must have been turned off. I kept waiting for the message to kick in, but the ringing never stopped. As a game, I counted the rings as I moved around my apartment waiting for an answer. On the forty-seventh ring, I finally heard a groggy voice answer. "Whassit?"

"Monique, it's Ben."

"Ben? Goway."

"You're the one who wanted to talk to me, remember?" I didn't even know if I was getting through to her, but I had to try. Maybe if she was half lit, she might tell me something she wouldn't disclose under ordinary circumstances.

"Too late. Too late."

"Too late for what, Monique?"

There was a hesitation, a sob, and then the connection broke. I'd have to try her again the next day; she was in no condition to share much of anything until she had a chance to sober up. As I got ready for bed, I couldn't help wondering what she'd meant by it being too late. Had it been too late to call, or was it something much more dire than that?

At 3:00 A.M., my telephone rang. I knocked the receiver off the stand in my stupor, and by the time I could say hello, the caller was gone. I debated hitting *69 to call whoever it was back, but I knew if I did that, I'd never get back to sleep. Most likely it was just Monique wanting some company for her drunken stupor. Well, she wasn't my girlfriend and never would be, and I'd taken no special vow to be her confidante, chum, or pal. I tried to salvage what little chance I had left at dozing back off and promised myself I'd deal with her in the morning.

It felt like I'd just gotten back to sleep when the alarm clock jarred me awake four hours later. I considered hitting the snooze button, but if I was going to help Louisa, I'd have to do it before the store opened. I had a busy morning planned helping my brothers fill an order, a big one that Mom had taken herself. In the afternoon, my class of neophytes met again for their second lesson. That left precious little time to sift through Jerry Sanger's troubles. I glanced out the window and saw that the rain had tapered off to a mist. It had to have been pounding down for the better part of the night, though. There was standing water in the parking lot of my complex, something that happened only after a long and steady rain.

I felt better after a long, hot shower, and as soon as I got dressed, I hit *69 to see if I could wake up whoever had called the night before.

I'd been expecting to hear Monique's groggy voice when the other party picked up, so I nearly dropped the telephone when I heard Kate's voice answer on the second ring.

"Louisa?" my sister asked anxiously.

"It's Ben. Somebody called me at 3:00 A.M. and then hung up on me. I never dreamed it could have been you."

Kate's voice caught a little, and then she said, "It wasn't me, but I've got a pretty good idea who it was. Louisa came over to spend the night. When I went to bed, she was safely tucked away in the guest bedroom, but when I got up an hour ago, she was already gone. Ben, I'm worried sick about her."

Kate had a tendency to worry about us all, but I hoped this time it was unfounded. "Relax, Sis, she's probably back at her apartment. You know how fierce Louisa is about holding onto her independence."

"You don't understand. Last night she told me how happy she was to be staying with us. Why would she leave without a word to me where she was going, and why would she call you in the middle of the night?"

Kate had me there. "Those are all good questions, but I don't have any answers."

"Will you look for her, Ben? Please?"

I wanted to tell her that I had to follow up on Jerry's life if I was going to help get Louisa out of Molly's crosshairs, but I couldn't do that if I was chasing my sister all over North Carolina. Then again, I needed to know what Louisa was up to, and if Kate's suspicions were right that she'd gotten herself into more trouble, I needed to intervene before it got any worse.

"I'll find her," I said. "Tell Mom I won't be in today until my class starts."

"I'll be happy to teach your class for you," Kate said.

"Thanks, I might just take you up on it. If I haven't tracked Louisa down by then, I'm going to have to call Molly. She's a lot better at this than I am."

"She may be, but she doesn't know Louisa like you do." She paused, then added, "Try the dam; I know she goes there sometimes to think."

"I thought they'd shut that road down months ago," I said.

"They did, but there's a back way by Fletcher's Pond that takes you right to it."

"I'd forgotten all about that," I said. "I haven't been that way since I was a teenager. I'll go take a look."

"Hurry, Ben. I'm afraid."

"She's fine, Kate, don't worry. I'll call you as soon as I find her."

"Bless you."

After I hung up with Kate, I grabbed my hiking boots from the closet. I hadn't been on that road in ages, but with the rains we'd been having lately, I was sure it would be treacherous footing. If there was one place in the world I didn't want to be slipping around in the mud, it had to be near the dam. What was normally a peaceful flow during much of the year could turn into roaring falls in an instant; I knew that from the past. If Louisa was going to hurt herself, something I tried not to believe, throwing herself into the raging river would probably be her style. Despite my assurances to Kate, I rushed out the door to search for my sister, hoping and praying that if she had decided to do something rash, I wouldn't be too late to save her.

FIVE

. . .

AS I drove near Fletcher's Pond, I spotted Louisa's Jeep parked in the brush behind the Granger's barn. I pulled my Miata right beside it, hoping I wouldn't need a tow truck to free my car from the muddy ground. I took a few seconds to change into my hiking boots before I climbed out into the mud, then I locked up the Miata, though I knew it wouldn't do much good if someone was determined to break in. Door locks on a convertible with a ragtop only keep honest folks out.

As I rushed up the path to the dam, I could hear the roar over the spillway long before I spotted the first glimmer of water. It started as a buzzing growl in the distance and steadily grew louder as I approached. By the time I could see the water boiling up near the edge of the dam, I wondered how the concrete and steel could hold back the force of the water as it pushed and shoved to get past. It was nearly to the edge of its containment. How long could it hold the torrent back? It took me a second to spot Louisa, perched on the edge of the dam itself. One pulse of water and the wave would sweep her down without hesitation. What was she thinking, risking her life in such a foolish way? Or was that the point? I shouted at her, fighting to get her attention, but my voice was drowned out by the thunder of the water. I tried waving my hands to catch her attention, but it was no use. Louisa stared resolutely at the water below her, and I felt my heart chill as I wondered if my sister was going to jump. I ran down the muddy path, the ground grabbing at my boots with every step, pulling me down, impeding me. It was as if the earth itself was fighting to keep me from my sister. I looked behind Louisa with alarm. A wall of water was rushing toward her even as I raced to Louisa. Surely it would reach her before I could. Why didn't she look up? Forcing myself to run faster, I rushed toward the dam, but I knew I was going to be too late.

"Louisa," I screamed again and again as I ran toward my sister.

Somehow I must have caught her attention, because she looked up at me while I was still a hundred yards away. The surge of water was closer to her than I was, and moving a great deal faster. I gestured behind her, but it took her precious seconds to understand. Suddenly she looked back, and I saw Louisa scramble off the dam and run toward me, her hat skittering off her head and landing in the spot where she'd been sitting. Louisa saw it, hesitated for a heartbeat, then abandoned it. By the time we met, the thrust of water had passed over the entire concrete rim, sweeping her hat along with it, burying it in the waves of froth and brown water far below.

She hugged me, and I could feel her shaking in my embrace. "Ben, I'm so sorry. Somehow my mind got lost in the water."

"It's all right," I said as I stroked her hair.

"Thanks to you. If you hadn't come along . . ." I saw her searching for her hat in the water below us, but it was gone, as if the river had swallowed it whole.

"You're okay, Sis. What were you doing out there on the dam on a day like this, anyway?"

"It's where I come to think. I lose myself in the water, and the sound of it. It is so powerful; it takes my mind off my troubles." She bit her lip, then said, "How did you know I'd be here?"

"I talked to Kate this morning. She was worried when you just disappeared this morning without a word to her."

Louisa said defiantly, "So she called our big brother to bail me out?"

I'd had about all the attitude from her I was willing to take. "Actually, I hit *69 and she answered. What was up at 3:00 A.M., and why didn't you stay on the line when I answered the phone?"

Louisa looked embarrassed. "I thought I wanted to talk, but when I heard your voice, I knew that I'd been wrong, so I hung up. It turned out what I needed was some time alone. That's when I got up, got dressed, and went back to my apartment. That didn't do me much good either, so I came here at first light."

"You shouldn't have taken a chance like that," I said.

"It wasn't that bad when I got here," she protested, and I knew it would be worse than useless to chide her about her foolish behavior anymore.

"Let's get you home," I said as we started the hike back to our vehicles. "You can skip work today. Everybody will understand."

"I'm not missing a minute of it," she said resolutely. "My only salvation in this entire insanity is working with the family and keeping busy. Being alone right now is the last thing I need."

I knew better than to argue with her, and besides, she

probably had a good point. "You still need to go home and change before work. You're a mess."

She said, "You're not exactly in pristine condition yourself, Ben."

I glanced down and saw that though I'd worn boots, the mud had still managed to splash up onto my pants. I'd have to change before I showed up for work, too, or Mom would have a fit.

"You're right. I'll meet you back at the shop after we both change our clothes," I said. We were at our cars, and before Louisa got into her Jeep, she hugged me. "I'm sorry I had a little snit back there. I was scared, and I took it out on you. Thanks for watching out for me," she said in a soft voice. It was rare enough for Louisa to apologize, and I knew better than to make light of it.

"Hey, what are big brothers for," I said as I returned her hug.

By some miracle I got the Miata free from the muck and the mire. I went home, changed clothes, and then headed to Where There's Soap before I took up the hunt again. Only part of the reason was because I wanted to make sure Louisa showed up and didn't just wander off again. I was in the parking lot the family used in back of the shop before I realized that I'd neglected to call Kate and tell her I'd found Louisa.

She was hovering near the back door when I walked in, probably waiting there for me.

Before she could say a word, I said, "Don't worry, I found Louisa and she's fine."

Kate nodded, and then I heard Molly say, "What do you mean, you found Louisa? I didn't realize she was missing."

Great, that was all I needed at the moment. "It was just a misunderstanding," I told her. "Louisa never was lost; she knew where she was all along." I hoped my grin would convince her to drop it.

Molly wasn't buying it, but I was in no mood to explain Louisa's perilous moments at the dam. Her actions could be too easily misinterpreted, especially given what had transpired the day before. It was time to change the subject, if I could. "So what brings you to Where There's Soap?"

She said, "I came by to talk to you. Do you have a minute?"

"Absolutely. Come on up," I said, leading her to my office. Kate shrugged an apology to me as Molly walked past her, but I gave her a brief nod of understanding. I hadn't given her much time or opportunity to warn me that the police were there.

Once Molly and I were in my office, I closed the door, just in case Mom came in. I wanted to speak to Molly in private, and we were in the only place in the entire building I could count on that happening.

"Any leads in your murder investigation?" I asked her.

Molly shook her head as she sat down in one of my chairs. "I'm not here to answer questions, Ben; I'm here to ask them."

That wasn't going to do at all. "Tell you what, why don't we trade off? That way nobody walks away empty-handed. You go first."

"Ben, this isn't a party game. I'm investigating a murder."

"And I'm trying to help my sister. The way I see it, we both have something at stake here."

Molly started to get up, and I knew I'd pushed her too far. There was nothing left to do but say, "Okay, you win. Ask away." Maybe I'd be able to get some kind of idea where she was heading by the questions she was asking. It was my only hope. I knew Molly well enough to realize she wasn't budging on this one.

Molly accepted my surrender and asked, "First, what

can you tell me about this?" She handed me a green leaf, one I immediately recognized.

"It's lemon balm. It's an antiseptic used in soapmaking. Where'd you find it?"

"It was in the victim's pant cuff. Is it rare?"

"Hardly. We have some growing in our herb garden out front, but you probably already know that, don't you?" Before Molly could jump to any conclusions, I added, "I'd be amazed if you found a soapmaking place that didn't grow some nearby."

"And how about this?" She handed me another small leaf.

"That's chamomile," I said.

"And you grow this, too?" she asked again, as if she was interrogating me.

"These are both basic ingredients in making soap, Molly. Would you like a tour of our garden? I can show you a dozen other plants we grow to use as additives. It's a lot cheaper than buying them from a supplier, we can be sure of the quality of the plants, and besides, the garden out front brings customers in."

Molly ignored my comment. "So Sanger could have picked these up here, is that right?"

There was no way I was going to let her focus on our shop alone. "I've already admitted that we grow both of those plants here, but I know I saw chamomile growing outside of A Long Lost Soap when I was there yesterday. I wouldn't be surprised if they had lemon balm there, too. It wouldn't even shock me if there was some growing near The Soap Bubble, or anyplace else that sells soap-making supplies. Why don't I go with you, and we'll check them all out together? I told you I might be able to help you."

She wasn't interested in my offer. "Thanks, but I should be able to recognize both of these on my own now. You were smart to admit you had these on the grounds. I already found them in your garden before you came in."

"Molly, do you still honestly believe Louisa had something to do with Jerry Sanger's death?"

Before she spoke, Molly looked out the window down to the sales floor below, and I saw her focus on Louisa as she stocked some of the shelves with herbs we dried. With a slight sigh, she said, "I'm just following my leads, Ben, wherever they take me."

I thought about sharing Monique's words last night, but decided that Molly would probably discount them without further evidence to back up my suspicions that she might have had something to do with the route salesman's murder. Besides, knowing Molly, she'd probably accuse me of interfering with her investigation, even though all I'd done was answer my phone.

"Is there anything else?" I asked.

She stood. "No, not at the moment. You don't heat with wood here, do you?"

Now what was that all about? "We have gas heat for the building. Why?"

"Does Louisa have a fireplace in her apartment?"

I couldn't imagine where she was going with her new questions. "You've got to be kidding; she barely has carpet. Why the sudden interest in Louisa's living quarters?"

She hesitated a moment, then reluctantly admitted, "Along with the leaves, they found wood ashes in Sanger's pant cuff."

"Sorry, I can't help you there."

She stood. "It was a long shot, but I thought you might be able to help."

"I earnestly wish I could," I said as Molly walked out. Wood ashes meant something specific to soapmakers, but I wasn't going to tell Molly until I had an idea how it applied to the murder. In the old days, they used to make soap by filtering rainwater through hardwood ashes to leach the lye. Based on an egg's buoyancy in the solution, they had a good idea just how strong the lye was. Only a die-hard soapmaker still went to the trouble to leach their own lye. Until I had the chance to look around more, I wasn't about to share that news with Molly, no matter how mad she was going to be when she found out I'd withheld information from her.

I decided it was time to talk with my brother Bob about the information Molly had given me through her questioning. That particular brother was truly a man of limited interests; for many of us, soapmaking was a career. For Bob, it was his life. My brother even went so far as to make soap on his days off using the old-fashioned methods. Sporting his ponytail and wearing one of his 1800s outfits, Bob was always a hit at craft fairs, demonstrating the old ways to anyone who would pause long enough by his iron kettle perched over an open fire. He'd even managed to talk me into some archaic soapmaking one weekend, down to the old cast-iron pots and simmering hardwood fires, but it just seemed like a great deal of work to me.

I found him in back staring at the production line, scratching his chin and frowning.

"What's up?" I asked.

"This equipment was ancient sixty years ago. The layout's all wrong; it should have been changed in the seventies. To top it off, they've stopped making some of the parts we need for so long that I have to forge my own sometimes."

I smiled. "Come on, you know that just gives you an excuse to get out your coal forge and anvil." Bob had become a rather accomplished blacksmith and machinist out of necessity, and it was a good thing he had. Otherwise we would have been forced to shut the production line down long ago. The equipment was just too expensive to replace, especially based on the revenues it brought in. To my continuing amazement, our boutique and classroom brought in a great deal more than our line in back, but I didn't know what my brothers would do without it. Bob might be able to teach a class now and then on old-fashioned soapmaking methods, but Jim and Jeff would be disastrous at it, and I couldn't see any of them waiting on customers up front.

Bob shrugged and said, "That's true, I love my forge, but I'd rather do it because I want to, not because I have to. Do you mind giving me a hand setting my equipment up in back? I've got to come up with a replacement for another broken shaft."

"I'd be glad to, if you've got time to talk while we do it."

Bob offered his crooked grin. "Bro, if you're willing to help me lift heavy things, I'll discuss the budget crisis in Washington with you."

I laughed, his good mood infectious. "It's nothing that mundane; I need some soapmaking background."

Bob laughed. "Are you telling me the great eldest child needs my advice? My heart's all aflutter."

I shook my head. "Don't get too excited. This is more up your alley. I'm talking about the traditional ways for making soap."

"Then I'm your man," he said as we moved his portable forge out back into a sandpit near the property line. I stepped back as Bob loaded the coal and coke into the forge, then watched as he started his fire. He didn't like to have his elbow jogged, I knew that well enough, so I just stood back and enjoyed the day. I knew winter was my brother's favorite time to work his forge, warming himself from the heat of the fire and the arduous nature of the work, but he was willing to sweat for the cause to keep the line going, and I admired him for it. At least Bob was getting a jump on it early. There was a slight breeze in the air, and it wasn't too uncomfortable yet, but I couldn't imagine standing anywhere near the forge in the heat of the day.

After it was burning to his satisfaction, he uncovered his anvil, a huge blackened hunk of iron mounted on a thick oak stump. With his tools laid out next to a few pieces of iron stock ready for the fire, it was time to talk again.

"So how can I help?" he asked. "Does it have anything to do with Sanger?"

"It might. Molly told me they found ashes in his pant cuff, along with some herbs that could have come from our garden."

Bob thought about that for a few seconds, then asked, "So you think whoever killed him was a soapmaker?"

I said, "Either that, or they want the police to believe they were. Do you know anybody in our area who still uses ashes to leach lye?"

Bob nodded. "I know half a dozen folks who do it. I've leached a couple of gallons myself in the past two weeks. Does that make me a suspect?"

It probably did if Molly knew about it, but I wasn't about to bring it up. She was well aware of how protective the brothers in our family were of our sisters, and it wouldn't surprise me a bit if every one of our names were on her list, including my own. Our past relationship and current friendship wouldn't cut me any slack, not if she suspected me of murder. "It doesn't make you one in my book, but I wouldn't admit it to Molly."

Bob shrugged, then said, "Who knows what I would have done if I'd known what was going on? I didn't like Sanger, but I wouldn't kill him. Not that way, anyway." My brother was so matter-of-fact in his statement that I believed him. I was certain he'd be able to come up with a much more creative way of dispatching the supplier if he had to. Bob looked at me a moment, then asked, "Did you tell Molly what the ashes could mean?"

I shook my head. "No, there's no way to be sure I'm right. After all, they could have come from somebody's fireplace."

Bob shook his head, and the disapproval in his voice was pretty obvious. "You're treading on dangerous ground, Bro. You know how she's going to react when she finds out you were lying to her."

"I never said a word to her that wasn't true," I protested.

He wasn't buying it. "Omission's just as bad as commission, you know that."

I hadn't felt like I had a choice at the time, but I wasn't going to stand there justifying my behavior to one of my little brothers. "I'll deal with that when it comes up. Any chance you can think of anyone who might have been dealing with Jerry Sanger *and* leaching their own lye?"

"Do you mean besides me? Let me think." He moved the coal around some with one of his handmade tools, then said, "I know the Kents over at A Long Lost Soap make their own lye every now and then. Melissa Higgins does, too. You know her, she runs The Crafty Corner."

"Since when has she needed soapmaking supplies from Sanger?"

"Melissa carries some of the basic soapmaking kits in her shop, and she uses scents in her candle kits. I know for a fact she and Jerry were friendly." Bob added, "I wonder if she was dating him, too?"

"From what I've been hearing, it wouldn't surprise me a bit. Anyone else? How about Monique White?"

Bob laughed. "Come on, Ben, you think the owner of The Soap Bubble's going to mess with homemade lye? I sincerely doubt it. I mean, can you see Monique grabbing a bucket of ashes and filtering rainwater through it?"

"Yeah, you're probably right." She might have used lye to

throw Molly off her trail, though. Monique certainly seemed capable of shifting the blame to someone else if she had to.

Bob poked the fire again, then said, "Listen, I'd love to chat, but I've got to get this thing forged before we can get started with today's run."

"Can I help?" I asked.

"No, this is a one-man job. I purposely came in early so Jim and Jeff wouldn't get in my way, and I don't need your fumbling help either." He grinned as he said it, and I felt a twinge of regret knowing my three brothers were closer to each other than they were to me. It wasn't just that they worked together every day. They'd been born fourth and fifth and sixth in line, and the three of them had been playing together since they could crawl; they had formed a bond between them that I couldn't touch. Louisa and I were close, and Cindy and I had a special tie—being the oldest and the youngest of our clan—but nothing like Jim and Bob and Jeff shared.

"I'll let you get to it then," I said as I patted my brother's shoulder.

Ignoring his forge for a moment, he said, "Thanks, Ben. Listen, don't give up on this. We're all counting on you to figure out who killed that weasel."

"I'm doing my best," I said, knowing that it was true, hoping that it would be good enough. At least my brother had given me another lead to follow.

I knew Melissa Higgins liked to open her craft store early in the morning, but not because I frequented her shop; it was on my walking route every morning before I went to work. I decided to pull the Miata off the road and walk the last hundred yards to her place. That way she wouldn't get suspicious when I showed up behind the wheel of my Miata instead of on foot.

The precaution was for naught, though. Her store was locked up tight, and there was a sign on the door that said, CLOSED FOR THE NEXT FEW DAYS. TRY ME AGAIN LATER. Since it wasn't dated, I had no idea how long the sign had been posted. It could have been up during my past walks and I hadn't noticed it. What can I say, I'm easily distracted. At one time, Cindy had walked with me so we could spend a little time together away from the shop, but it hadn't lasted long. She was a power walker, always going all out swinging her arms and pumping her legs, focused on making good time. Me, I liked to stroll, stop and look around if the occasion merited it, checking out a bird in the sky or a tree branch that grabbed my attention along the way. We'd both just ended up frustrating each other, and I'd happily gone back to my solitary walks. I couldn't help wondering if the sign had been put up before Jerry Sanger's death, or just after. It seemed the ripples of the man's murder were spreading farther and farther from the moment I'd found him on our doorstep.

There was nothing I could do except promise myself a return visit later. Since I was already away from the soap shop, I decided to drive over to Monique's and see if she made any more sense sober than she had stone drunk the night before. She had to be experiencing the world's worst hangover right about now, and that was fine with me. I wanted her off balance when I questioned her, and doing so through a pounding headache might be my best bet to get the truth. As I drove to The Soap Bubble, I wondered about Bob's admission that the Kents made their own lye. Had they passed on that skill to Heather? The granddaughter, though she didn't look like a murderer to me, had every reason Louisa had to want Jerry Sanger dead. But could she have killed him? Heather seemed as sweet as she could be, a real Southern girl bred with genteel manners and softly spoken words. But I'd been raised by a Southern Mamma, with three Southern women as sisters thrown into the mix, and there wasn't a man alive who knew the strength and capable manner of Southern women more than I did.

When I got to The Soap Bubble, I thought Monique might have defied tradition and opened her shop early.

Then I saw that the lock had been broken as the door swung slowly open in the breeze.

SIX

. . .

"MONIQUE," I called out as I stepped cautiously through the door. "Are you here?"

The second I was inside her shop, I knew something terrible had happened. Spilled aromas, the essences of a hundred different ingredients, assaulted my olfactory senses as I walked in. Crushed and powdered herbal additives were strewn all over the floor, making a nasty paste that clung to my shoes as I walked through the pristine surface of the spill. "Monique? Are you here?"

I heard a groan in back, and rushed to the sound. I found Monique under a shelf, part of the heavy cherry wood pinning her to the floor. I tugged on the shelf, straining against its bulk, and finally managed to set it upright again.

When I looked back at Monique, I didn't like what I saw. There was a terrible gash on her forehead and the skin around it was crusted with crimson. She must have lost a lot of blood before the wound had stopped bleeding, if the stains on the floor were any indication. From the dried edges of the cut, I imagined she'd been there awhile. Worse yet, there hadn't been a flicker of movement since I'd found her, and I felt my heart freeze in my chest. I couldn't bear the thought of her dying on me, not with what had happened the day before on the back steps of my family's soap shop.

I almost couldn't believe it when I saw her eyelids flutter, and then open. She looked completely disoriented as I knelt down and reached out to comfort her with my free hand. "Hang on, I'm calling an ambulance." After telling the 911 operator about the situation, I closed my phone and we waited. After a minute, I had to ask, "Monique, what happened here?"

"Water," she croaked out. I couldn't see how it could possibly hurt to give her a sip, so I hurried back to the kitchenette and filled a glass from the tap.

"Hold my head," she said as she struggled to get up.

"You shouldn't move." I knew how serious a neck injury could be. I'd seen some straws in the cabinet near the glasses and retrieved one.

"Sorry, it's the best I can do."

She took a single sip, then started to cough as I pulled the straw away. "That's enough for now. Do you feel up to talking?"

Her eyelids fluttered as she said, "Attacked. Too late. Couldn't stop it."

"Come on, you're going to be all right. I promise you that. Who attacked you? Did you recognize them?"

She seemed to lose interest in our conversation, and I didn't have the heart to push her any more than I already had. I heard the sirens in the background, and in less than a minute the EMS unit was there. As they checked Monique, I heard another siren. Just don't let it be Molly, I thought in a silent prayer.

No such luck.

She wasn't all that happy to see me when she walked into the shop. "Ben, I wish I could say I was surprised to find you here."

There was nothing I could really say but, "Hi, Molly."

She looked around the shop in disgust. "With the way you tracked this mess up, there's no way we'll get a decent footprint here. As a crime scene, it's as contaminated as it could get."

"She needed my help," I protested as the techs pulled Monique out of the shop, her head and neck strapped to their carrying board. "I thought it was more important to see if I could keep her alive than make it easier for you to investigate what happened here. Sorry if I messed things up for you." I shouldn't have been so angry, but I was being flooded with emotions, and I couldn't seem to keep my mouth shut. Only after I'd scolded her did I realize I was taking it out on the wrong person. She hadn't done anything to deserve my barking.

"I know, you're right," Molly said. "It's just frustrating to keep finding you one step ahead of me."

"You know what? I'm the one who's sorry. I didn't plan on this happening. She called me last night, and I came by to see what she wanted. To be honest with you, she was pretty drunk, and I half expected to find her here hung over. If it helps, she told me she was attacked before she lost her focus."

"I can imagine that," Molly said as she looked around. "It's a real mess, isn't it?"

Suddenly I remembered the clear surface of the spill when I'd arrived and said, "Getting here first wouldn't have done you any good, anyway. There wasn't a footprint in the entire mess."

"Ben, think about it. Are you sure?"

I recalled the pristine spread of powder on the floor. "I'm positive. Sorry I couldn't be more help."

She smiled. "But you just were."

"How's that?"

She explained, "It makes sense, along with what Monique told you. This was probably an assault made to look like a break-in. That tells us quite a bit. She's a lucky woman: I have a feeling her assailant didn't expect her to survive."

"And you can tell that how?" Then it hit me. "If the break-in had happened first, there would have been tracks on the floor when I got here. Monique was assaulted, then the spill was made to divert suspicion."

Molly said, "Very good, Benjamin."

I shook my head. "But it still doesn't make any sense. Why would anybody come after Monique?"

"That's the next question we need to ask her," Molly said.

"We?" I asked.

She raised one eyebrow as she stared at me. "We as in the police, not we as in you and me. Are we clear on that?"

"Yes, Ma'am." I started to leave, but before I could get out the door, Molly asked, "Ben, are you positive you don't know why she called you last night?"

"I had a feeling she wanted to trade soapmaking recipes," I said with a smile.

"Now why don't I believe that?"

I shrugged, then said, "I guess you're just not as trusting a soul as I am."

I wanted to root around in Monique's life more, but I had a feeling Molly would be treading those grounds in heavy boots. I had to find another avenue to check. The note on The Crafty Corner's door intrigued me. Surely if Melissa Higgins had planned to be gone long, she'd have found a substitute to run her store. At the very least, she would have taken time to make a classier sign. I decided to go back and see if I could find the name of her alarm company. If it was the same one we used at Where There's Soap, I might be able to wheedle some information from them. Dan Trenton, the man who operated Eye Spy Alarm, was a crusty old goat who rarely let his left hand know what the right one was up to, but if I could convince him I needed the information, he might give me something to go on.

To my surprise, Melissa's store was open when I went back to check on the alarm company. I certainly hadn't expected to find the lights on and the CLOSED sign taken down. Her shop was filled with sections on just about every craft imaginable, and I wondered how in the world she'd ever mastered so many different disciplines. I'd been making soap all my life, and I still didn't consider myself an authority on the subject.

I walked in and found her at the cash register restocking her till. She was a heavyset, middle-aged woman who obviously enjoyed her personal freedom, evidenced by the brightly colored clothes she always chose to wear. At the moment, her flaming red hair was offset by the purple and blue swirls of her peasant dress. "I thought you were closed."

"Hi, Ben," Melissa said, "I just got back a few minutes ago. I've been gone three days, and I loved every minute of it. The Blue Ridge Parkway was stunning, I absolutely adore going there in the summer. I drove up through Virginia and had a blast. I even dropped in a little on the Skyline Drive while I was up that way. I hate to admit it, but I wasn't looking forward to coming back." She hesitated, then added, "Maybe I need a change of scenery. I've been thinking about closing the store and relocating to a different part of the world. Do you ever get wanderlust, Ben? You must, with that huge family of yours. What do you say, want to hit the road with me and see what there is to see?"

I laughed, as the spirit of the offer intended. "Had you planned the trip for long?"

She shook her head, smiling all the while. "You know, that's one of the joys of owning my own business and not caring if I run it badly. I can put a GONE FISHING sign up whenever I feel like it. So why are you here? Did you need some craft supplies?"

This was the part I hated, and I was beginning to wonder if I'd ever be free of the burden of sharing this particular piece of bad news. "No, but I've got to talk to you. Have you heard about Jerry Sanger?"

Melissa grinned. "Oh yes, I've known about his dalliances for some time. Don't tell me he finally got caught. How delicious. Tell me more."

There was no other way to put it, so I said, "Somebody killed him on the steps of our shop yesterday."

Melissa acted as though she didn't believe it at first. "You're kidding, right? That's not even funny as a joke, Ben."

"I wouldn't kid about something like that."

Melissa frowned, then said, "Why Ben, that's just terrible. Who would do such a thing?"

"That's what I was hoping you might be able to help with."

Melissa looked startled by the statement. "Me? How could I possibly know anything about something that happened at Where There's Soap?"

"He was your supplier, too, wasn't he?"

Melissa finished stocking the register and closed the drawer as she said, "It was nothing like what he carried for you folks. I saw him once a month. We chatted off and on, but he never made a pass at me. I used to wonder why he wasn't interested, since he was going after every other woman in sight. Not that I would have done anything about

it, you understand, but still, a girl likes to be asked every
now and then." Melissa added, "That's just terrible news.
Did they catch the killer yet?"

"No, the police are still looking. Say, Bob told me
you've caught the soapmaking bug."

Melissa gave a short bark of laughter. "Your brother has
a tendency to exaggerate. I've played with it some, but I
like to spread my hobbies around. That's why I opened this
shop. I've tried my hand at weaving, crocheting, candlemaking, model building—I even built my own rockets with
those cute little engines. This place is a playground for me.
Say, I've got something you might like."

She leaned over and retrieved a ship-in-a-bottle kit. "You
should get one of these. I understand they're very relaxing."

It was the last thing on earth I wanted to do. "Thanks,
but I've got more than I can handle now."

"If you change your mind, I've got dozens of projects
around here." She grinned, then added, "I don't carry many
soapmaking kits, though. I'm willing to leave that to you
experts."

"Thanks for your time, Melissa. I'll see you later."

"Think about my offer," she said, laughing. As she retrieved a dainty watering can for indoor plants, she said,
"Bye, Ben. You know you are welcome here any time. Now
I must see to my little indoor garden. I'm afraid I've been
quite negligent lately."

I left Melissa to her plants and headed out to my Miata,
wondering where I should go next. Bob had said that the
Kents leached their own lye at one time, and I wondered if
their granddaughter Heather had acquired the skill, or
some of their production run. At the very least, I wanted to
look around and see if they had the herbs found on
Sanger's body growing around the shop. I hadn't had the
chance to explore Monique's place when I'd been there,
but I'd have to swing by there later. No doubt Molly's

crime scene investigation was going full force, and I didn't want to step on her toes again if I could help it.

HEATHER startled me by smiling as I walked into A Long Lost Soap, but that disappeared the second she recognized me. It had taken her a few seconds to realize that I wasn't a customer looking for something to buy. Funny, I thought I was more memorable than that. As her smile faded into a frown, I said, "Now is that any way to be?"

Her words were short and clipped as she said, "Mr. Perkins, what brings you back to my grandparents' shop? I thought we were finished with our business."

I shook my head and offered her my most insincere smile. "Heather, I'm just getting started. Have the police interviewed you yet?"

"Briefly," she admitted, "but I'm more than willing to speak with them any time they're interested in talking to me. I want to see the killer caught and punished as much as anyone else does." She had put all of her emphasis on "them", no doubt to let me know that my questions weren't all that welcome since I was a civilian, just like her. That was just too bad if she didn't like it. I wasn't there to be popular; I was trying to clear my sister.

I said casually, "I notice you have chamomile and lemon balm growing outside." I'd paused long enough at the door to confirm my earlier suspicions. Knowing the Kents, there had been little doubt in my mind they'd find a patch of ground to plant some herbs in, even if it meant digging up the sidewalk in front of their shop, and I'd been right.

She frowned at me again, and I almost told her that if she didn't stop that, she was going to have a face like a road map in twenty years. In a condescending voice, she said, "Certainly we do. My grandparents believe in only the freshest ingredients for their soaps."

I wanted to tell her to save the sales pitch for her customers. "Does that also include freshly leached lye as well?"

"It does," she said. I'd gathered as much by the ash bin out back when I'd been snooping around before going inside the shop itself. It was amazing what you could find out if you didn't mind getting caught.

Trying to keep my tone conversational, I asked, "Do you leach any lye yourself?"

She nodded. "I have in the past." Tersely, she asked, "Is there a point you're trying to get to, Mr. Perkins, or are you one of those dreadful middle-aged men in love with the sound of their own voices?"

Now that stung. "Hey, I'm in my early thirties; I haven't hit middle age yet, at least I hope not. And what happened to Ben? I thought we'd graduated to first names."

She bit her lower lip, then said, "Listen, I understand what you're trying to do for your sister, but I've already told you, I can't help you, and I'm not about to give you anything you might try to twist into something against me."

I shrugged. "Fine. I'll let the police officer in charge of the investigation know that you're finished talking to me. I'm sure she'll be willing to give you more attention herself than you've been getting so far. Have a nice day."

As I started for the door, Heather called out, "That's not what I . . . I didn't realize . . . What else can you possibly ask me?"

I was stretching the truth that I would talk to Molly about our conversation, but I hadn't broken it, since it was still a possibility, no matter how remote. Since Heather had been emphatic about being finished talking to me, I was actually considering telling Molly about the ashes, and the young woman's response. If Heather leaped to the conclusion that I was working on the case with Molly, I couldn't do anything about that.

I took a deep breath, then said, "Frankly, I'm not satisfied with your explanation about your relationship with the victim."

Heather frowned. "I told you before, we dated, but it was never anything all that serious. I didn't know about the other women in his life, but I wouldn't have minded. It wasn't a big deal."

I didn't buy that for a second, not from the way she'd reacted when I'd first told her of Jerry Sanger's fate. "Does that imply that there are other men in your life as well?"

She stiffened, and I thought she was going to throw me out, but after a few seconds Heather calmly said, "There aren't any other men, at least not anymore. I've decided to go back with my old boyfriend. I never realized how good I had it with Hank until recently."

"Good for you," I said. "When did you decide that?"

"Yesterday," she said. "Is that all?"

"All I can think of at the moment. Thanks for your time."

She nodded absently, and I decided to leave before she banned me from the store for life. I'd tried to stir things up with her, and I'd managed, at least a little, but she hadn't broken down with a confession. Neither had Monique, and I'd had her dizzy from a head trauma and hung over to boot. The only confession I'd heard that day was from Melissa, and she'd cheerfully admitted to having no relationship with Jerry Sanger whatsoever. As I left the Kents' shop, I headed back to Monique's business. If Molly was still there at The Soap Bubble, I planned to confess my interview with Heather to her and offer to exchange information. If she wasn't there, it might be the perfect time to do a little snooping on my own. The circumstances around Monique's troubles were unsettling, and I had the feeling someone may have been trying to get rid of her before she had a chance to come clean.

Molly's squad car—along with all the others—was gone when I drove up. I parked in the lot next door and walked around to the back of The Soap Bubble. The Miata was pretty easy to identify as mine, and I didn't want anybody to know I was there snooping around. At first I couldn't find the herbs in question. There was a garden plot in back of her shop, but it was overgrown with weeds and volunteers, making it tough to identify anything but morning glory vines in the mess. The garden hadn't been tended to in at least a couple of years, and I wondered why Monique had ever bothered. Then I spotted a row of pots in her back windowsill, including the two varieties I'd been searching for. But there were no ashes, at least none that I could see. I was looking inside a couple of cans under the back porch when I felt something hard nudge me on the shoulder.

In a voice I knew only too well, I heard, "Find what you're looking for?"

I turned and gave Molly my brightest smile. "I have now that you're here."

From the expression on her face, charm alone wasn't going to get me out of this. "Can it, Ben, what are you doing?"

"Looking for ashes," I confessed simply. It shocked me as I uttered the absolute truth to her, but what other reason could I give?

"So you finally decided to share that little tidbit with me, did you?"

Busted. "Are you telling me you knew what the ashes meant all along?"

A slight smile cracked her grim expression. "Not at first, but I started looking into lye production, and that led to the history of it, and we both know where that ended up." The grin faded as she added, "Why didn't you tell me the truth earlier?"

"I wanted to talk to my brother Bob first," I admitted. "He's the resident family expert on the subject, and I'm not all that up on leaching."

"He's a good source to have, isn't he? Your brother filled me in right after you left him, and I could tell it wasn't his first question about lye today."

Molly had dug in faster than I could cover my tracks. I was suddenly glad I'd decided to come clean with her.

I nodded my agreement. "Yeah, but did he tell you that the folks who run one of the other soap shops still use lye, including their granddaughter, who happened to admit to me that she'd been dating Jerry Sanger?"

Molly started to cloud up, and I added quickly, "Hey, I came to you first with this, didn't I?"

She shook her head and bit her lower lip, a sign I recognized as agitation beyond the norm. "Ben, I just found you digging through trash cans. Are you going to have the audacity to stand here and lie to me as well?"

It was time for a little indignation. "Hey, I resent that. Okay, so I decided to swing back by here first before I talked to you, but you were the next stop on my list."

"I'm sure that's the case," she said.

"Molly, I've never lied to you, not directly. I'm not saying I haven't kept things from you in the past, but I've never intentionally deceived you."

She shrugged. "I suppose that's true enough."

"You know it is," I said.

"Don't get self-righteous with me, Benjamin Perkins, you know as well as I do that you can lie just as easily by not saying a word."

I shrugged. "I was going to talk to you next. It's the truth, take it or leave it."

Molly accepted it, then said, "So what else did Miss Heather Kent have to say for herself?"

"She told me she was getting back together with her old boyfriend. She actually tried to convince me that she was dating Jerry on the side just for fun."

Molly shook her head. "I wonder about her definition of fun. Listen, is there anything else you're holding back? I mean anything. I need to know, and I need to know right now."

I wasn't about to tell her about Louisa at the dam, and I'd already come clean about everything else. Well, almost. I might as well make a total sweep of it.

"There's one more thing. I found the herbs you discovered on Jerry Sanger's pants at two other soap shops, but it's nothing to go on. There were even herbs growing in the borders outside The Crafty Corner, and plants inside the store, too. Chamomile and lemon balm aren't exactly exotics, you know. It seems like everywhere I go, I'm seeing them. It's the white truck syndrome."

"What are you babbling about now?" she asked.

I'd had this discussion with my brother Jeff a few days before. "We tend not to notice something until it's significant to us. The next time you drive down the road, count the white trucks you see. I'm willing to wager you'll find them everywhere, but if I hadn't just mentioned it, you'd never have noticed them."

"You've lost your mind completely, you know that, don't you? I do have to admit that I'm seeing herbs everywhere I look. They're turning up in the oddest places." She gestured back to The Soap Bubble, then added, "We didn't find any here, though. I had a man search the grounds this morning."

"Did you have him look on the windowsill?" I asked, pointing to my discovery.

She looked where I was pointing, then said, "No, he must not have thought of that."

It was time for a question of my own. "Did you happen to find any ashes inside Monique's place?"

"No, but then again, we missed the plants, didn't we? I'm going to have a talk with Pickers; he should know better than miss something so obvious."

"I've got another question. Have you heard how Monique is doing?" I asked, remembering the gash on her forehead.

"I checked in five minutes ago. She broke her wrist when the bookcase fell on her, and the cut on her head took nine stitches." Molly added, "The hangover didn't help matters. She admitted to tying one on last night." Molly scratched the dirt with her shoe, then asked, "You got to her before anyone else. Did she tell you what happened?"

"No. I figured she might have said something to you."

Molly said, "The only thing she remembers is the shelf hitting her from behind. Still, it's probably a good thing you found her when you did. That head wound could have been a lot worse."

"I'm just glad I could help. So what are you going to do now?"

"That's police business," she said automatically, then added, "but since you gave me the tip, I'll tell you. I'm going to go have a conversation with Heather Kent."

"Want some company?" I asked. "She just loves having me around."

"I thought you had a soap shop to run."

I laughed. "Are you kidding me? Between my mother, my brothers, and sisters, not to mention my grandfather, I'm amazed they still keep me around."

"Me too," she said. "Ben, I meant what I said. Stick to what you know best."

When I didn't respond, she said, "You're doing it again, aren't you?"

"What's that?"

"Lying to me by not opening your mouth."

I just smiled, and after a second she shook her head and walked away. I went with her and said good-bye as she drove off. I wasn't about to promise I was finished snooping. Louisa was still a suspect in Molly's mind—she would have told me otherwise if she was having second thoughts—and as long as my sister was under the microscope, I wasn't about to back off.

If only I could figure out a place to start stirring things up again.

I headed back to Where There's Soap, hoping that something else had come up, anything that might help me clear Louisa. If it didn't, I'd grab some lunch, teach my class, and get back out there.

It was the only thing I could do.

SEVEN

∘ ∘ ∘

I walked into Where There's Soap ten minutes before my class was ready to begin. Not wanting to leave my lunch to chance again, I'd grabbed a burger on the way in this time. I knew better than to go through the drive-through window, but I was in a hurry. I'd asked for a hamburger loaded with everything but mayonnaise; I'd said it twice. So what did I get? Mayonnaise only, and a lot of it. At a stoplight I scraped all of it I could off the bun, but it still had a lingering taste that ruined the quick meal for me.

When I walked in the door, Mom said, "What's wrong, Benjamin? Has something else happened?"

"No, I just got reamed at the drive-through," I said.

She shook her head. "That's what you get for eating fast food. You should do something about your diet, Benjamin."

I patted my stomach. "That's easy enough, since I'm not on one." Sure, I was ten or twelve or fifteen pounds over-weight, but unlike Molly, I wasn't doing anything special to fight it besides walking every morning before work. I added, "Besides, every time I try to lose weight, you tell me I'm too skinny and bake more treats."

Since she wasn't about to admit that she ever did anything to add to my weight gain, Mom changed the subject. "Have you learned anything new since the last time we talked?" she asked.

"Monique White was just attacked in her shop," I said. "I'm the one who found her." A look of concern swept over my mother's face, so I hastily added, "Don't worry, Molly said she's going to be okay."

"What is this world coming to? Was it because of what happened to Mr. Sanger?"

"I honestly don't know, and if Molly suspects it, she's not saying."

Mom looked at me triumphantly. "Call her right now, Benjamin, she needs to be here. We can prove Louisa is innocent."

"And just how are we going to do that?"

Mom said, "I know for a fact that your sister stayed with Kate all night, and she's been here all morning. We can offer her a perfect alibi."

I hated to wipe that happy expression off my mother's face, but she couldn't go around proclaiming Louisa's alibi, particularly when she didn't have one. "Mom, we don't know when Monique was attacked," I said. "And besides, she wasn't at Kate's the entire night."

"What do you mean?" Mom asked sharply. I was on thin ice with her, but I didn't want to betray my sister's trust, either.

"No one was with her on her way to Kate's house, and she left before Kate did this morning. I'm not sure how long ago Monique was attacked. I'm not even sure she knows herself."

That got me a steady scowl. "Benjamin, your sister no more hurt that woman than she killed Mr. Sanger."

"Hey, don't take it out on me. I believe that, too," I said.

"Then prove it, Benjamin."

"I'm doing my best." I glanced at the clock and said, "Sorry, I've got to go."

"Following up another lead?" she asked.

"No, I've got the second session of my class to teach."

Mom frowned, then said, "So let Cindy take it. She would love to start teaching, and it's time we let her spread her wings a little."

To the contrary, I knew that my youngest sister dreaded the prospect of standing up in front of a class more than anything in the world. Cindy had told me that herself when she'd pawned this class off on me, but she was afraid to tell Mom. I didn't mind, since I enjoyed teaching, but it proved that my mother didn't know everything her children were up to at all times. That was a good thing; it probably saved her a dozen heart attacks a year.

"No thanks, I want to teach it myself," I said.

"You're as stubborn as your father was," Mom said.

I kissed her cheek. "That's the nicest thing anybody's said to me all day."

"Go, teach your class. But when you're finished, I expect you back on this, Benjamin."

"Yes, Ma'am." It was all I could do not to salute.

I headed for the classroom, wondering what I could do to investigate that I hadn't already tried. Molly was ready to lock me up for meddling too much as it was, and Mom didn't think I was doing enough. There was no way I was going to be able to please both of them, but I was going to have to try.

Herbert and Constance, my most vocal students, were already in the classroom when I walked in.

"You two are early," I said as I started gathering materials for the day's class.

Herbert said, "She wanted to come an hour ago. It was all I could do to keep her from standing in line before you opened up this morning."

Constance said, "Herbert Winslow Wilson, you know full well you're enjoying this every bit as much as I am."

He winked at me out of her sight, then said, "Well, it's better than that crocheting class you dragged me to last year."

"You're the one who made the afghan," she said smugly.

Herbert's ears reddened. "I had to do something with all that yarn you bought. There was enough to cover the Statue of Liberty."

From the sound of it, I figured this could go on for hours, and I had a class to prepare for. "What have you got there?" I asked, pointing to a few soaps in front of them.

"We made these last night," Constance said. "Only we had some problems."

I picked up a bar and unwrapped it. The smell of lavender nearly knocked me over.

Constance said, "It's too strong, isn't it?"

I was choking on the fumes as I hurriedly wrapped the bar back up. "How much did you use?"

"The whole bottle," Herbert said proudly. "My mother used to wash with lavender-scented soap. I think it's just right."

"That's because your nose is as bad as your ears are." She turned to me and said, "So what's your expert opinion?"

I wasn't about to dash Herbert's first solo effort away from class, but I had to handle it carefully. "Whoever uses this won't soon forget it was handmade."

Herbert said, "There, you see? He agrees with me."

"Are you daft, man? He said nothing of the kind."

Before they could ask me anything else, the rest of the

class came in. "Are we too early?" a lively older woman asked as she walked in. I searched for her name in my mind, but I didn't have a clue. I could remember a face from a dozen years before, but names were always my downfall. That was why I insisted my class wear name tags. Louisa had designed a batch in the shapes of floral soaps, and most folks delighted in adorning and personalizing their tags. Thankfully, I said, "Come on in, Helen." I'd spotted her name tag at the last second, and she looked pleased by the personal acknowledgment.

I knew Herbert was getting ready to continue our earlier discussion, so I said, "Excuse me, I need to get things ready now."

He looked particularly displeased with me for dodging him, but I'd keep dancing as long as he pursued it. After all, I'd told them myself that soapmaking was highly personal. I just pitied the person who received one of Herbert's soaps as a gift. It would take me a week to get the lavender scent off my hands, and I hadn't even washed with it.

When I had everything ready and the seats were all filled, I said, "Okay, let's get started. Yesterday we learned the basics of melt-and-pour. Today we're going to play a little. We've got two basic forms of dye. There is the powdered type we add directly to the mix, and we also have color nuggets. The dye in the nuggets has been partially diluted, then added to a soap base."

"What's the difference?" Herbert asked.

I held up a baggie in one hand and a few colored nuggets in the other.

"This is the powder," I said, shaking the bag. "And these are the color nuggets," I added, gesturing to the other hand. The class tittered, and I added quickly, "But beyond that, there's no real difference in how we use them. It's more a matter of preference than anything else."

Herbert wasn't about to let it go. "Then which one is easier to use?"

"You can't go wrong with color nuggets," I said, and Herbert nodded his approval.

I continued, "We also have an array of choices for scents that can be added. Feel free to use the charts posted on this wall to get just the blend you want." I gestured to the combinations Cindy had made up. She had the best nose for combining surprising ingredients to create a unique scent. "The bottles are all clearly marked, but remember, a little goes a long way." I avoided Herbert's gaze as I said, "These combinations have proved to be successful in the past, but feel free to make up your own."

"How about layering and swirling?" Helen asked.

"Somebody's been studying," I said, and Helen grinned. "That's where a lot of the fun begins." I held up examples as I explained, "You can add a darker color and drag it through your initial melt with a toothpick or a fork. You can also pour a layer, play with it, then add another on top of it, changing things as you go. We've also got chilled cubes of different soaps you can add to yours to give it a really unusual look. We'll be covering those techniques more thoroughly in a later class, but if you feel like playing today, be my guest."

"Why do the shapes have to be chilled?" Herbert asked.

"Remember, the soap base is hot when it's melted down, and we don't want to lose the shapes we're adding. Chilling them helps keep their form."

Herbert nodded. "Makes sense."

"Another fun thing to do is to make a small layered shape by pouring some of a dark soap mix into a plastic pan, then embedding cookie cutters into the blend and letting them harden in the refrigerator. When they're chilled, you can use them in your soaps as an embedded object. Kids particularly seem to love that."

That got a good response. Did any kid ever wash up enough for their elders? My class was beginning to see some practical applications to their new hobby. I said, "Your only limit is your imagination. Now let's have some fun."

I roamed through the room as they worked on various projects, enjoying the infectious laughter my students shared as they worked. Even Herbert seemed to be having a good time, something I took as a very good sign. He might have been a curmudgeon on the outside, but it was obvious he enjoyed learning something new as much as the schoolkids I taught now and then.

When it was time to wrap things up, I said, "Again, feel free to shop around the store now that we're finished. Before you go, make sure your creations are clearly marked so I'll know which soaps belong to you. Thanks again for coming. I'll see you all tomorrow."

They were all well pleased with themselves as they headed into the boutique, and I took a second to walk around to see what they'd done. There were some wonderful pieces there, along with some that wouldn't pass a kindergartner's inspection, but the important thing was that they had all had enjoyed creating their masterpieces. That, more than any finished product, was the barometer I always used for success.

As I walked out of the classroom, Cindy rushed up to me. "I was just about to interrupt your class. There's an urgent call for you, Ben."

"Who is it?"

She shook her head. "All I know is that it's from the hospital."

I picked up the telephone and identified myself.

A pleasant contralto voice said, "Mr. Perkins, my name's Stacey Vance. One of my patients is pretty adamant about seeing you immediately. Is there any way you could come by the hospital?"

"Who's the patient?" I asked, though I suspected I knew.

"Sorry, I should have mentioned that. Her name is Monique White. She's pretty agitated, and to be honest with you, all the floor nurses would really appreciate it if you could come by."

"Hang on a second, Stacey," I said.

I covered the receiver, then said, "Cindy, I know how much you hate messing with a class, but is there any way you could wrap up their soaps and distribute them after the soaps harden?"

"Why? What's going on? Who's in the hospital?"

"It's Monique White, and I think she might be ready to tell me something about what happened to her."

She nodded. "Go, Ben, I'll handle things here."

"Just wait half an hour, wrap their soaps up, and turn them all loose. Thanks, Sis."

"No problem. I just hope Monique knows something to help you. We all want you to get Louisa out of this, Ben. You realize that, don't you?"

I patted my youngest sister on the shoulder. "I do now, knowing you're even willing to take my class for me."

She stuck her tongue out at me, and I winked in return. "Tell Mom where I went, would you?"

"Just go," she said. Cindy was the youngest of our brood, just out of high school. She still wasn't sure soapmaking was what she wanted to do with her life, but she'd decided to give it a year to see how she liked it. Mom was pushing her to go to college so she could get a degree in accounting to help out with the books, but Cindy had other ideas. I'd back her in whatever she decided. Since Dad died, she'd looked to me for support, and I always did my best to deliver.

I grabbed my keys on the way out, but not before announcing to my class milling about, "My sister Cindy will take care of your creations and dismiss you. It was a great class today."

As I hurried to the hospital, I wondered what kind of bombshell Monique was going to drop in my lap.

THE nurses were certainly thrilled to see me when I walked onto the hospital floor and identified myself. I hadn't had that kind of reception since I'd hit a grand slam in Little League baseball. I knocked on Monique's door, and I heard a subdued command to enter from inside.

She certainly looked a great deal better than she had when I'd found her that morning. The blood had been cleaned from her face, and her hair had been combed down to cover as much of the bandage as possible, though I could still see the bruise starting to color up below it. Monique's wrist was in a cast, but other than that, she looked fine. Her hair was brushed and she'd even managed to apply her makeup before my arrival.

Her smile was warm and inviting when she saw me, and I could feel the power of her attention directed fully onto me. "Ben, thank you so much for coming."

I saw flowers on her nightstand and on the windowsill, then I realized I shouldn't have come empty-handed. "Sorry I didn't bring you anything."

"Nonsense," she said, "your presence is all I need. Please, sit down."

I sat beside her bed and said, "I must say, you're looking well."

"You're kind to say so," she said as she primped at her hair with her good hand, "but I know how ghastly I must appear. You're too kind to say otherwise."

We sat there another thirty seconds in silence, then I asked, "The nurses said you wanted to see me?"

"I needed to talk to you, Ben." She reached out her good arm toward me and offered her hand. I took it, though it made me feel slightly uncomfortable. Monique and I had always had a rather sharp relationship, and I couldn't help wondering what had suddenly softened her up, unless that blow to her head had done more than the doctors knew.

"Ben, thank you for saving my life."

I protested, "Come on, I didn't do a thing. I just dialed 911 and the doctors did the rest." I pulled my hand away, hoping it wasn't too abrupt an act. If she minded, she didn't say.

Monique wouldn't hear of my denial. "Don't be so humble. If you hadn't come along when you did, who knows what might have happened to me?"

"What exactly did happen?" I asked. Hopefully Monique was feeling generous enough to tell me the truth. It would certainly help my standing with Molly if I could actually report something back to her.

Monique said, "The police have been determined to find that out for themselves. Believe me, no one is sorrier than I am that I couldn't help them."

I sat on the edge of my chair. "You don't remember anything that happened?"

She shrugged, then winced slightly as she accidentally moved her broken wrist. "As I told them, I opened the shop earlier than usual this morning since there were a few things I wanted to get accomplished before my clientele started to arrive. I went to the mailbox to put some bills out, and someone must have slipped inside when my back was turned. In seconds I felt the shelf crash down on me, and the next thing I knew, you were ministering to me."

There had to be more to it than that. It was time to push a little harder. "What could they have been after? Do you have any idea?"

"I honestly have no idea. I make my deposits every night, and I keep just enough cash on hand during the day to make change. Believe me, it's no fortune." She gestured to her arm and forehead. "If they'd wanted my meager funds so badly, I would have gladly handed everything over to them."

"So you believe it was an attempted robbery?"

She looked startled by my suggestion that it could have been anything else. "What other reason could it possibly have been? I haven't made an enemy in my life, at least not that I'm aware of. Why do you ask?"

It was time to say what I'd been thinking since I'd found her pinned under that bookcase. "I was just wondering if this had anything to do with Jerry Sanger's murder."

She said, "Do you honestly believe that someone's killing soapmakers and their suppliers? I can't fathom that happening."

"Monique, maybe you know something you don't realize is significant. Could you be a threat to the murderer in any way?"

She paled at the theory. "I don't see how."

"Think about it. It's worth considering."

She lay back on her pillow and said, "Ben, I'm afraid the strain of your visit has been too much for me. Do you mind leaving me now?"

I stood and said, "Not at all. Listen, if you do think of anything, call the police. They might be able to help."

"And deal with that insufferable woman again? She's unbearable. I won't stand for her snide tone of voice, do you hear me?"

"Then call me and I'll tell them." I could let Molly know myself, though I knew she wouldn't enjoy hearing something about the case secondhand. Still, finding a lead would make up for it. I hoped.

"Promise me you'll call if you think of anything," I said.

"For you, I will. Good-bye, Ben. Thank you for coming."

I was outside her room when one of the nurses approached me. I saw by her name tag that she was Stacey, the nurse I'd spoken to on the phone.

"You're leaving so soon?" Stacey asked.

"She decided she wasn't up to visitors," I said. "Has she been a real pain?"

The light over Monique's door came on, and I could hear a buzz at the nurse's station nearby. Stacey just shook her head as she said, "I'd better get that. Come back any time."

I saw Stacey bite her lip before going into the room. It appeared that Monique hadn't gone out of her way to make any new friends during her stay at the hospital. So why had she really summoned me to her bedside? I had a feeling there had been something she'd wanted to tell me when she'd called. I wondered what had changed her mind in the time it took me to get there. I still wanted to know what she'd been babbling about the night before when she'd been drinking, but she'd thrown me out before I'd had the chance to ask that. I'd pushed a little too hard, and I'd been tossed out on my ear for my trouble.

So where did that leave me? Monique looked more and more like another intended victim of Jerry Sanger's killer. There was just no way I was going to buy the robbery coincidence. Why Monique, though? Was someone going after her rivals after she'd taken care of the lothario himself? If that were true, I wondered how long it would take Molly to focus on Louisa again. Then it struck me that if the killer was going after Jerry's other lady friends, Louisa had to be pretty high up on their list. I dialed the shop's number on my cell phone as soon as I was outside. After having Kate patch me through to Jim, I told my brother, "Listen, I need you and Bob and Jeff to keep an eye on Louisa."

"What's she going to do, party tricks?"

"Jim, this is serious. Monique's been hurt, and I'm starting to wonder if somebody is going after Jerry Sanger's other girlfriends."

"Got it. Don't worry, we're on it." Jim hung up abruptly,

and I felt immensely better. My brother may not have been the world's most diplomatic fellow, but I knew when it came to our family, he wouldn't let me down.

Not having Louisa to worry about left my mind free to consider the other possibilities. I needed to dig a little deeper into Jerry Sanger's love life, as repugnant as the idea was to me. So who knew him the best? Did he have any drinking buddies? Was there someone he played tennis with? There had to be a male friend somewhere, but how was I going to track him down? I considered calling Molly and asking her, then rejected the idea just as quickly. Most likely she wasn't in the mood to share that kind of information with me. I couldn't very well call Jerry's boss, but then a thought struck me. I could call one of his competitors. After all, I knew some of the suppliers hung out together after hours. Maybe one of them could help.

IT took four phone calls and two dead ends before I finally tracked John Labott down. John supplied us with molds for our soaps, a range of sizes and shapes that was truly staggering.

"John, this is Ben Perkins."

His voice was easy and affable, a perfect salesman's pitch. "Hi, Ben. Are you out of molds already? Funny you should call; I've been meaning to stop by your shop. I've got a new line that's going to knock your socks off."

I wanted to talk to him, but I wasn't about to ambush him during a sales call. "Come by some time next week and I'll have a look. The reason I'm calling isn't about business, though. Well, not entirely. Not at all, I guess."

"Okay, I'm intrigued. What can I do for you?"

"There's something I need to know. How well did you know Jerry Sanger?"

He hesitated, then said, "Yeah, I just heard about what happened to him. We weren't exactly friends, but we got along okay."

I had been hoping for more than that. From the tone of John's voice, I doubted he'd spent any more time around Jerry Sanger than he'd had to. "Do you have any idea who his best friend was?"

John took some time to think about my question, then said, "I don't know much about his personal life. Do you mean in the business? Well, I'm guessing it had to be Steve Erickson. They were always drinking together at Suds whenever I was in there." Suds was the name of a bar thirty miles from Harper's Landing in a town named Fiddler's Gap. "Why, what's up?"

"It's not that important. I was just curious."

John said, "So why are you nosing around? That's not like you. Oh no, please tell me they don't think Louisa had anything to do with this."

Now how did he know that? "I won't lie to you; she's a suspect at the moment."

John snorted in disgust. "That's crazy. She never should have been with him in the first place. Your sister was way too good for that snake."

"You know that, and so do I. Truth be told, she probably did, too. There wasn't much I could do to stop her though. You know my sister; she's always had a mind of her own."

John hesitated, then said, "Listen, if there's anything I can do to help, and I mean anything, all you have to do is ask."

There was something I'd suspected for years, and now was as good a time as any to ask. "John, you like her yourself, don't you?"

He blustered a little, then finally said, "I'm fond of your entire family, Ben."

I wasn't about to let him off the hook that easily. "That's

not what I mean, and you know it. John, why didn't you ever ask her out yourself?"

He sighed, then admitted, "I did. Once. She shot me down."

"Give her a few weeks and try again. I've got a feeling she might be more receptive this time."

"I don't know," he said. "I might seem like this outgoing guy when it comes to selling, but in my personal life, I'm pretty shy. It takes a lot for me to get my nerve up."

"Suit yourself," I said, "but isn't it worth a try?"

He paused a few seconds, then said, "Maybe. Yeah, maybe it is. See you soon, Ben."

"Good-bye, John, and thanks for your help." So Sanger hadn't been the only supplier interested in my sister. Louisa had opted for the wrong man, in my opinion. Sure, John wasn't as flashy or as smooth as Jerry had been, but those were points in his favor, in my opinion, not against him. I'd have to mention something to Louisa about the fact that John might ask her out. I wanted her to think about her response before she even heard the question.

I got Erickson's cell phone number from Cindy back at the shop. After she gave me the number, I asked, "So how did it go with my class?"

"Come on, Ben, even I could handle that much."

"Hey, I know you could do it all. I'm just sorry I put you in that position."

Cindy started to say something when I heard Mom's voice behind her calling her name. "Gotta go. Bye."

"Bye," I said, then called Steve Erickson. I got his voice mail saying he was finished for the day and that I should leave a message.

I had a pretty good idea where he'd be, thanks to John's tip. It was probably close to drinking time for Steve Erickson, so I decided to drive over to Suds and see if I could track him down.

At first I thought I was at the bar too early. The place was just starting to fill up, but I couldn't find Steve among the late afternoon drinkers. I was just about to give up when I saw him saunter out of the men's room. He spotted me before I could approach him.

"Ben Perkins, I didn't know you drank here," he said as he slapped me on the back hard enough to jar my fillings.

I tried to generate a little enthusiasm in seeing him myself, but I wasn't as good a salesman as he was. "There's a first time for everything, isn't there? I was running an errand for the shop and decided to duck in for a beer. Can I buy you one?"

He said, "I haven't turned a free one down yet, and I'm not about to start now." He held two fingers up to the bartender, and a few seconds later we had a pair of glasses in front of us. I paid the bartender, a heavyset man with a bushy beard, as I tried to decide how to handle Steve. I'd been all set to interrogate him when I'd stepped into the bar, but I decided to use his mistaken impression to my benefit.

I held my glass up toward him and said, "Here's to Jerry Sanger."

"To Jerry," Steve said, and then he drank deeply, killing half of his beer with one extended swallow.

"It's a sad thing, isn't it?" I asked after I'd taken a much more moderate sip.

"Truer words were never spoken. It's an absolute shame." He spun his glass around on the coaster in a seasoned move that I guessed he'd had a lot of practice at.

I took another small sip, then asked, "Any idea who might have done it?"

"I've got a theory or two."

"Anything you'd care to share with me?" I asked.

"I'm not really sure why you're asking me." He drained the rest of his beer and ordered another. I'd barely touched mine, but he signaled the bartender for two more anyway. Maybe he was going to drink them both.

I pushed a little harder. "I'm curious, aren't you? Who do you think killed him?"

Steve took a healthy swallow of his fresh beer, then said, "You know something, Ben? You're the last person in the world I should be talking to about this."

"Why do you say that?"

He snorted once. "Come on, he was dating your sister, along with half a dozen other women on his route."

I took another sip to buy some time, then said levelly, "Hey, Louisa's a big girl. What she did in her personal time was none of my business. So Jerry had a lot of girlfriends, did he?"

Steve shrugged. "Let's just say our old pal Jerry was fond of dating the women on his route. Not me; that's a sure way to get yourself in a bind. I never mix business with pleasure."

"Do you know anybody in particular he was seeing—besides Louisa, I mean?"

He stared at his beer for a few seconds, then said, "It would be a shorter list to name the ones he wasn't making time with. You know, I really shouldn't be talking about this with you." He finished his beer, then said, "That's my limit, I've got to be heading out."

"Where are you off to? I've got some time on my hands. I'd like to discuss your other theories with you." I couldn't let him get away, at least not until I got some specific names from him.

He slapped me on the shoulder again, even harder than the last blow. "Sorry, Pal, maybe another time. Right now I've got a big date with a waitress at the bowling alley down the street. See you around."

I didn't let go of his arm.

"Tell me who you suspect fast, then." I didn't want him

to leave before I at least had an idea what he was talking about.

"You're persistent, aren't you? Let's just say Jerry had his ladle in lots of different pots and leave it at that. Now like I told you, I'm late." He pulled away from my grip, and I let him.

"Good-bye," I said. It appeared that Steve Erickson didn't have the slightest idea what he was talking about. Coming to Suds had turned out to be just another dead end.

The bartender approached and asked, "Can I get you anything else?"

"No, I'm set."

He wiped the bar down and made Steve's empty glass disappear, then finally said in a near whisper, "I wasn't eavesdropping, but I nearly choked on that toast of yours."

"Why, weren't you a big fan of Jerry Sanger?"

"Jerry was all right," the bartender said. "It just burned me the way Erickson matched glasses with you."

"Why's that?" I asked.

He looked around, then leaned across the bar toward me. "Four days ago, I heard him threaten to kill Jerry right where you're sitting. Kind of a coincidence that Jerry turned up dead, isn't it?"

I felt my skin prickle. "What were they arguing about?"

"What do you think? It was over some woman, near as I could make out. I didn't catch a name, but I had to slam my baseball bat down on the bar to get their attention. And now he's toasting the man's memory! He's got a lot of nerve, if you ask me."

I thanked him for the information and bumped up my tip before I left even though I left a full beer there in front of me. It was time to head back to Harper's Landing. The drive to Where There's Soap flew by; I had plenty to think about along the way. Steve Erickson had just made it to my list of suspects, and he was climbing high with everything

I heard. Had his little comments about Jerry been his way of taking suspicion off his own behavior? He might have had more reason to wish his competitor harm than he'd been willing to let on. I couldn't keep what I'd just discovered to myself, but I had no idea how I was going to tell Molly exactly how I'd come by my new information.

I didn't have much time to think about it when I got back, either. Molly's squad car was in front of Where There's Soap when I drove up, and I knew I had to tell her the second I saw her.

EIGHT

∘ ∘ ∘

I was surprised to find Molly standing on the front porch when I drove up. Normally I parked in back with the rest of the family, but I could see that she wouldn't like it if I did that, so I whipped the Miata into a spot beside her squad car.

As I approached her, she said, "So the wanderer returns. Ben, have you given up soapmaking altogether?"

"There was somewhere else I had to be," I said.

For a second I thought she was going to ask me what I'd been up to, but for some reason it appeared that she'd changed her mind. "I bet. So how was Monique?"

"Which one of my darling siblings told you where I was this afternoon?"

She laughed. "Don't be so paranoid. A cop spotted you going into Monique's room and called me. It's still my case, too, remember? So what did she have to say? From the way I heard it, she was making everybody in sight miserable, and then you showed up and charmed her."

"What can I say—it's a gift I have to use with caution."

Molly didn't laugh; she didn't even smile at my joke. "And she said . . ."

"Do you want the truth? She wanted to thank me for helping her," I said.

Molly didn't look like she believed it for a second, but I wasn't about to elaborate.

Finally she said, "You were certainly gone a long time just visiting Monique."

I thought about keeping the bartender's tip about Steve Erickson to myself out of sheer cussedness, but changed my mind the second it occurred to me. It was, after all, Molly's job to follow up on the lead and not mine.

"I did find something out that might be a help," I said.

"Benjamin Perkins, I told you to stop digging into this." Her cheeks were flushed, and from her stance, I could tell she was honestly upset.

"I wasn't looking all that hard," I said, "but you're right, it's none of my business. I'll leave you to it. Sorry I said anything."

I tried to walk past her, but she stepped in front of me. "You know better than that. Give."

I didn't like her tone of voice, and I'd never been a big fan of taking orders from anybody. "You know what? You could be a little nicer about all this. I thought we were friends, or have you forgotten about that completely?"

Molly took a deep breath, then said, "This is a murder investigation. I can't tiptoe around you just because we date sometimes."

"Molly, I'm not looking for any special consideration here. Just treat me with the courtesy you would a stranger and we'll be fine."

She nodded. "That shouldn't be hard; I've never met anyone stranger than you." Though she'd tried to joke her way out, her tone and manner with me still stung. I was beginning to wonder if I'd ever ask her out again after the way she'd been behaving lately.

"Don't make me say please, Ben," she said.

"Okay. I stopped off at Suds, you know that bar in Fiddler's Gap? While I was there, I ran into a guy named Steve Erickson. He's one of our suppliers, too, and we had a toast to Jerry's memory."

"Is there a point to this somewhere?"

"Give me a second, would you?" Now I was really getting irritated. True, I was trying to help save my sister's hide, but did that mean Molly had to be so stiff-necked about the whole thing? "After Steve left, the bartender told me that Erickson had threatened to kill Sanger four days ago, right in front of him."

Molly took a notebook from her breast pocket and said, "Steve Erickson, you say? Do you happen to know where he lives?"

"No, but I've got his company name and his cell phone number. I didn't get the bartender's name either, but he's a pretty big guy with a bald head and a full beard; he's kind of hard to miss."

"Okay, that I can use. I'll look into this."

As she drove away, I called out, "You're welcome," but she was already gone. I never did find out why Molly had been out to Where There's Soap in the first place. I guessed it wasn't as important as the lead I'd just dropped in her lap.

The shop was just closing as I walked in. Cindy was at the door switching the sign as I crossed the threshold.

"So how's the competition?" she asked.

"I couldn't say; I didn't realize we had any. Oh, you're talking about Monique? She's going to be fine. From the sound of things, she's back in her usual foul mood, so she must not be feeling all that bad." I looked around the store and saw Mom in her office upstairs going over the day's receipts with Kate. No doubt Bob, Jim, and Jeff were in back shutting down the line. That left one sibling unaccounted for. "Where's Louisa?"

"She's in the break room with Kelly."

"Has something new happened?" Molly's visit to Where There's Soap might not have had anything to do with me after all.

"Molly wanted to question her again, and Kelly insisted on being here for it. They've been holed up back there most of the afternoon. In fact, Molly just left."

"Yeah, I ran into her outside."

I lingered around the break room door, pretending to straighten the shelves as I waited for them to appear. After ten minutes of checking the same stock half a dozen times, the door opened and both women walked out. Louisa was smiling, a good sign if I'd ever seen one. I said, "Hello, ladies."

"Hi, Ben," Louisa said, then turned to Kelly. "I'll talk to you tomorrow."

"You can count on it," Kelly said.

After my sister was gone, I asked Kelly, "Are there any new developments?"

"Now, Ben, you know I can't discuss anything going on with the case," she said as she shook her head slightly, smiling at me the entire time.

"And I wouldn't dream of asking," I said, returning the smile and acknowledging that I'd gotten it.

Kelly looked at her watch and said, "Is it that late already? I'm starving; I skipped lunch completely."

Out of politeness more than anything else, I asked, "Do you and Annie have big plans tonight?"

Kelly frowned. "She's visiting her father. I don't know what I'm going to do without her around. I always miss her when she's gone."

Suddenly I didn't feel much like eating alone, either. "Would you like to grab a bite with me? I was just getting ready to go out and get something to eat myself."

She studied me a few seconds, then said, "Are you asking me out, Ben Perkins?"

I shrugged. "Why not? We both have to eat, don't we?"

Kelly smiled. "I have to say I've had more eloquently worded offers in my time, but a hungry gal can't be all that choosy, can she?"

"Hey, I've got no problem with you settling for me. So where would you like to go?"

Kelly hesitated, then asked, "How about the Lakefront Inn? I hear their new chef is wonderful."

The Lakefront was a little steep for my budget, but I could swing it if I ate a brown bag lunch every day for the next few weeks. "Then the Lakefront it is."

"Good, let's go. I'm starving."

Cindy was grinning at me as I walked past her, and I scrunched an eyebrow at her, daring her to say a word. All she managed was "Have a nice meal" as we walked out.

When we were out on the front steps, I asked, "Kelly, should we both drive, or would you like to ride with me?"

She didn't even have to think about it. "Oh, let's take the Miata. I've wanted to ride in it since I saw you tooling around town one day with the top down."

"It might get a little too chilly for that tonight," I said. The evening was unseasonably cool, and I knew firsthand how chilly it could be driving around with the top down.

She put an arm in mine as we walked to my car. "Come on, where's your sense of adventure? I'm game if you are. We should enjoy the cool weather. How often do we get it in the summer?"

Once we were at the car, I reached into the glove box and took out a woman's scarf. "You might want to put this on then. The wind won't blow your hair so much."

She studied the floral print, then said, "Well, I see someone who's in touch with his feminine side."

"It's not mine. I mean it is, but it's not like I wear it or anything. Oh, just put it on."

She laughed as I put the top down. It was a sound full of life and exuberance. With the scarf around her head, Kelly said, "Okay, I'm ready. Let's go."

As I drove, I said, "I've been trying to get Molly to consider somebody as a suspect besides Louisa, but I feel like I'm beating my head against the wall."

Kelly touched my arm. "Ben, is it all right with you if we don't talk about the case tonight? I haven't been out to dinner in ages, and I'd like to just enjoy the evening, no business talk at all, if you don't mind."

"Certainly."

When we pulled up into the restaurant part of the inn, the place was nearly deserted. I said, "I hope they're open tonight."

She glanced at her watch and said, "Ben, it's only six. I'm sure their dinner crowd doesn't start gearing up until after seven."

"Would you like to drive around a little longer then? We could go out into the country; it's beautiful in the convertible."

She jumped out of the car. "Are you kidding? I'm famished as it is. We can take a drive later. Come on, let's go."

I smiled softly, enjoying Kelly in this new light. When she'd been in my soapmaking classes, she was always focused and intent on learning, and when she'd been with Louisa, I'd seen the competent professional she was. Now I was seeing a completely different side of her, a young woman set to have fun. Her mood was infectious, and I found myself hurrying to catch up with her before she made it inside.

The inn had been built in the 1800s, and I'd always

been a fan of its architecture. The clapboard siding was painted in a soft golden yellow hue, and the forest green shutters and door looked perfect. There was a rose garden between the restaurant and the inn, and a walking path between the two with stepping stones melted into the grass. Inside, the restaurant sported broad heart-pine board floors, and the ceiling was all fine wooden beadboard. Old-fashioned wallpaper with flowers and curlicues covered the walls in a background the same shade of gold as the exterior. The tables were all of an elegantly simple Shaker design, and fine linen covered them. The crystal shone in the light, and I multiplied the number of days I'd be eating out of a sack by twenty. The look on Kelly's face was worth it, though. There were half a dozen folks spread throughout the dining room, and I realized most of them had to be guests at the adjoining inn, given the barren look of the parking lot.

Kelly said, "Oh, this looks wondrous."

A short little man with a broad black moustache said, "Will there be just the two of you?"

"That's right," I said.

Kelly said, "A table by a window, please."

He nodded. "But of course."

He led us to a table with a beautiful view of the nearby garden, and I managed to grab Kelly's chair and hold it out for her just before he beat me to it.

She thanked me, then studied the menu for a few moments before speaking. Finally, Kelly said, "Let's see, what looks good. I'm going to start with a shrimp cocktail, then maybe have a filet mignon. I've been craving red meat for weeks. Annie's trying to turn me into a vegetarian, and my darling daughter is driving me crazy with her campaign." Kelly looked at me and asked, "What are you having? Go wild, Ben, it's my treat."

"I'm the one who asked you out to dinner, remember? I can pick up the check."

Kelly frowned. "We're not going to have any of that nonsense, are we?"

"I don't know what you're talking about," I said stiffly.

Kelly rolled her eyes. "Okay, first, I backed you into this dinner invitation; there was no gracious way for you to refuse. I admit it: I was shameless. I couldn't bear the thought of eating alone tonight, and I thought you'd be good company. Was I wrong?"

I smiled. "Oh, is that it? Do I have to sing for my supper if I don't pick up the check? Are we going to have an impromptu soapmaking lesson with the dessert course?"

She laughed. "No shoptalk, yours or mine, I promise. I want to see if we can get through the evening without mentioning soap or the law. Agreed?"

"Agreed. The least we should do is got Dutch, though. It's not fair for you to pay for my meal."

"Oh, please. I want to. You're not going to take that pleasure away from me, are you? If there's one thing I can't stand, it's Southern macho pride."

I said, "You don't have to twist my arm. You can get the check, if I can cover the tip. There's nothing macho about the request, but it's not negotiable."

"So if you can't leave the tip, dinner's off?"

I shrugged and said, "It's your decision," as the waiter approached. Kelly crinkled her upper lip, her eyes never leaving mine, as she said to the waiter, "We'll need just another minute."

"Of course, Madam. Whenever you're ready."

I matched her gaze, until finally she said, "You'd have made a heck of a lawyer, you know that?"

"No shoptalk, remember?" I said. "So what's it going to be?"

She laughed, then nodded. "Be my guest. The tip is all yours."

"Then let's get that waiter back over here, I'm starving, too."

After a wonderful meal full of good food and even better conversation, Kelly and I both reached for the check at the same time. She said, "Ben, I thought we agreed."

"How am I supposed to know how much to tip if I don't see the total?" I asked. One look at the bill told me I was glad I'd lost that particular argument. After we settled up and walked outside, there was a definite chill in the air. I started to put the top back up when Kelly said, "Can we leave it down? I want to see the stars."

"It's going to be cold, but I'm game if you are. I've been known to drive around with the top down in the snow."

"That must be great fun. Come get me the next time it's snowing, promise?"

"It's a date," I said as I got in. "Would you still like to take that drive?"

"Absolutely," she said.

"Then let me grab a blanket from the back." The trunk space wasn't much, but it was large enough to hold a fleece blanket I kept back there for just such occasions. I couldn't believe the declining temperature at this time of year. I handed the blanket to her and said, "Use this, it'll help with the chill."

"What about you?"

I said, "I expect you to share, young lady. We can work it around the stick shift."

She laughed and waited until I was buckled in before giving me part of the blanket. As we drove, we talked about things large and small, some of great consequence and some of none at all. Later, I caught Kelly yawning, and said, "I'm not putting you to sleep, am I?"

"No, it's not you. I was up at five this morning getting Annie's things together, and I'm beat."

"We're not far from the shop now," I said. "I can have you back at your car in no time."

When we got there, the parking lot was empty save for her car. I took the blanket and stowed it back in the trunk as she put the scarf back in the glove box.

She said, "I can't remember the last time I had so much fun with another grown-up."

"It must be tough raising your daughter by yourself."

Kelly said, "It's the only way I'd have it." I walked her to her car, and she surprised me before getting in by leaning forward and kissing me. It wasn't much more than a peck, but I felt a charge from it nonetheless.

As Kelly opened the door to her car, she faced me and said, "We need to do this again."

"That sounds great to me, if you're willing to get the tip next time."

She smiled, then said, "So now you expect me to pay for the entire meal?"

"No, I meant we'd switch next time and I'd get the check," I stammered.

"I knew exactly what you meant, Benjamin." There was a light in her eyes I hadn't seen before, and I hoped that I'd been partially responsible for putting it there. "This may be forward of me, but who cares? I'm free tomorrow night. Annie will still be at her dad's."

"Tomorrow it is then," I said.

We were still standing there when the spotlight hit us from another car I'd missed, parked in the shadows. I held my hand up and said, "Who is it?"

"It's Molly," she said.

"Shut the light off, would you?"

"Sorry," she muttered, then joined us a few seconds later.

"What's going on?" I asked.

"I was out patrolling and saw an empty car in the lot. With what's been happening lately, I thought I'd better hang around and see who it belonged to."

Molly nodded to Kelly, then added, "Sorry to interrupt."

"You weren't interrupting anything," Kelly said. "We were just saying good night."

The three of us stayed like that for nearly a minute before Molly said, "Well then, I'd better get back to work."

After Molly drove away, Kelly said, "I'm so sorry about that."

"About what?"

"I forgot all about Molly being your girlfriend. I shouldn't have kissed you like that."

I took Kelly's hand in mine and said, "Listen to me carefully. Molly's not my girlfriend. We're friends who go out on occasion, but we're not in any kind of relationship beyond that."

Kelly looked at me steadily for a moment, then asked, "I can tell you believe that, but does she know that?"

"If she didn't before, there shouldn't be any doubt in her mind now."

Kelly hesitated, then said, "Does that mean we're still on for tomorrow?"

"I'm still interested if you are. Tell you what, why don't I cook for you instead of us going out?"

Kelly nodded, buzzed my cheek, then said, "That sounds wonderful. Good night, Ben, and thanks again."

"Thank you," I said.

After she drove off, I walked up to the steps of Where There's Soap and sat there staring out into the night. Molly had indeed acted jealous upon finding me with Kelly, but she'd been just as adamant as I'd been when we'd decided to keep our relationship uncommitted. We'd have to find some way to work through it. I couldn't lose Molly as a friend—she was important to me—but I wasn't about to give up the growing excitement I'd felt being with Kelly. Somehow we were all going to have to work things out. Having Jerry Sanger's murder hanging between the three of us didn't help matters, but no matter how angry Molly got with me, there was no way I was going to back off on that. I had a feeling that if I kept digging, I'd uncover who had really murdered Sanger. As interested as I was in Kelly, and as important a friend as Molly was, I had a priority that outranked them both. My main job for the next few days and weeks was to find a way to get my sister Louisa off the hook.

I just hoped I'd be able to focus the next day and not spend it thinking about my date tomorrow night.

NINE

∘ ∘ ∘

THERE were four messages waiting for me on my machine when I got home. Under ordinary circumstances, I could go two weeks without getting that many calls. I sat by the machine and hit Play, wondering why I'd suddenly become so popular.

Cindy's voice was the first one in line. "Ben, you've got to call me the second you get in; I don't care what time it is. Don't you dare call Kate first, you hear me? I want to hear all about your date tonight. Bye." It hadn't taken long for two of my sisters to start speculating on my evening. Well, they'd just have to wait till morning to hear what I had to say, if I told them anything even then. After all, just because we were family didn't mean they had to know all my business, though I'd have a tough time convincing either one of them that was true.

The second message was from Molly. In an abrupt tone of voice, she said curtly, "Sorry about tonight. I was out of line." I definitely had to spend some time repairing the fresh rips in our friendship. At the moment I wasn't exactly sure how I was going to do that, but it was important to me, so I'd find a way.

My heart quickened when I heard Kelly's voice leaving the third message. "Hello, kind sir, I just wanted to thank you again for a wonderful evening. I'm already looking forward to tomorrow night. Sweet dreams." There was a warmth in her voice that I loved hearing. It was funny how quickly my attitude toward Kelly had changed. When she'd been my student in soapmaking classes, I'd enjoyed her presence, but I never really thought about asking her out. I'd heard the rumors that she wasn't interested in dating, and I hated being turned down asking for dates, something I'd carried with me since a particularly disastrous rejection in high school. But it looked like the rumors might have been wrong. Kelly and I had meshed from the start, even enjoying the moments of silence that were usually deadly during a first date. There was some real potential there, something I hadn't felt in a long time.

The fourth message brought me out of the warm glow like a bucket of cold water poured over my head.

It was delivered in a low grating whisper, and I couldn't tell for the life of me whether it was from a man or a woman. The message was clear enough, though: "Back off or suffer the consequences."

I called Molly on her cell phone, something she'd told me a dozen times was for emergencies only. This counted, in my book.

"Molly, it's Ben," I said when she answered.

"Geeze, do we have to do this tonight? I said I was sorry. Can we just leave it at that?"

Trying to keep my voice even, I said, "It's not about that. Listen to this message that was on my machine."

I hit Replay, then fast-forwarded through the first three messages. I stopped too quickly though, because we both heard Kelly's warm good-bye. Molly said, "So you've got a new girlfriend. Congratulations. Why are you calling me, Ben, to rub it in?"

"You know I'd never do that. Listen." The machine played the threat, and Molly said softly, "Rewind it. I want to hear it again."

I did as she asked, making certain I got to the beginning of the fourth message and not the end of the third. The words chilled me again as I heard the repeated threat.

Molly hesitated, then said, "Okay, don't erase that. I'll be right over."

Fifteen minutes later she showed up at my apartment. I'd had time to brew fresh coffee, and I made some of the almond-flavored stuff she preferred. If she noticed it when she took her first sip, she didn't say anything about it.

After she took a sip, she said, "Let's hear it one more time. It lost something over the phone."

I was expecting her to want to hear it again, so it was all cued up and ready to play. After the whispered voice finished its brief threat, Molly said, "Ben, I'm going to need that tape from your machine."

I certainly wasn't crazy about that idea, especially given the first three messages I'd received. "That was the fourth message on my machine. The other three are kind of personal."

Molly looked at me sternly. "Okay, we've got one from the creep, one's from me, and one is from your new attorney friend. Who's the other one from?"

"It's from my sister Cindy."

She shook her head. "And you're worried about that

right now? I can't even fathom what that's about, but I know how you are about your privacy. Here's what we'll do. I'm willing to let you keep your tape if, and it's a big if, we can get a clean recording off it."

"Honestly, I'm not trying to be a pain. I just don't want you to have to deal with all this other stuff, given our history."

Molly said, "If that's really all you're worried about, I'm going to go ahead and take the tape. I'm a big girl, Ben. We've said we're nothing more than friends all along. This was bound to happen to one of us sooner or later. It just happened to you first."

I didn't like the edge in her voice as she spoke. "Slow down, Molly. In the first place, being friends is pretty important in my book, and in the second place, nothing's happened, at least not yet. I'm not even sure our dinner tonight was a real date."

Molly's eyebrows shot skyward. "Don't kid yourself, I saw the way Kelly was looking at you." She added hesitantly, "I guess I was kind of caught off guard finding you two together like that, but I'll be fine, trust me."

"To be honest with you, it kind of surprised me, too." I stood close to her and kept her gaze. "Is this going to be a problem for us?"

She hugged me briefly, then said, "Not if we don't let it."

"You're sure we're good?"

She said, "We're good. Now can I have that tape? I want my people to listen to it."

"Aren't you worried about what they'll say about the message you left me? It doesn't exactly put you in the best light."

"There's not much I can do about that, now is there?"

If she could handle the heat, then so be it. I took the tape out of the answering machine and handed it to her, then I put in a spare I had in my handheld recorder. I'd bought them both for just that reason, because they used the same size tape.

Molly tucked the tape into her shirt pocket and said, "If I were you, I'd take the advice on this tape."

I gestured toward her as I said, "Let me ask you something. Would you stop digging just because somebody threatened you?"

"You don't get it, do you? The difference between us is that I'm a trained peace officer and you're a soapmaker. Leave the crime solving to me."

There was something she wasn't considering, but I'd hesitated to bring it up, given the current tensions between us. "Molly, I must be getting close to something. Why else would I get a message like that?"

"Can you give me anything more specific than that? I don't even know all the places you've been digging. Is there any way you can narrow the list down to a manageable number?"

I thought about it a few seconds, then realized that if I'd given someone reason to try to scare me off, I had no idea who it was. "No, I've been stirring every pot I can find, hoping something would happen."

She said, "Well, if you're not careful, something's going to happen, but it's going to be something I guarantee you're not going to like. Stop taking chances, Ben."

I looked into her eyes and could see the earnestness in her message. "Is that a cop talking, or my friend?"

"It's both. I've already been to three funerals this year, and I'm in no mood to go to a fourth. I'll talk to you later."

I let her out, and Molly tried the door as soon as I shut it.

"Did you forget something?" I asked as I opened it back up.

"Aren't you even going to lock this thing?"

She was worse than my mother. "I always do, right before bed."

"Let me hear it latch, or I'm going to have to babysit you all night."

"I can take care of myself," I said.

"Throw the lock, Ben."

I did as she asked, throwing the dead bolt as soon as the door was closed. Through the door, I called out, "Are you happy now?"

"Ecstatic," I heard her say.

After she was gone, I tried to figure out who I'd gotten close enough to in the last two days to ignite anything like that threat. I'd talked to Monique White, Heather Kent, Steve Erickson, John Labott, Melissa Higgins, Kelly, Molly, and all of my family, though if any of them were going to threaten me, I doubted they'd do it anonymously. I thought about Louisa—she'd been on edge lately—and that incident on the dam made me realize my sister was under a lot of pressure. But could there be any possible reason in the world that would make her kill someone and threaten me? I just couldn't see it. I knew Molly or Kelly wouldn't have left that message, each for their own and very different reasons. I supposed that any of the others could have done it, though I'd have a tough time figuring out the motive for a few of them. So where did that leave me? In a way, it was positive news. Chances were good that I'd already talked to the killer. Why else would they threaten me? That made the suspect list much more manageable, regardless of what Molly thought. So which one of them was it?

I still hadn't come to any concrete solutions by the time I fell asleep. Tomorrow it would be time to stir the pot again. I was hoping I could come up with something a little more specific to use that would help me eliminate at least one of the suspects on my list.

* * *

THE next morning there was a car I didn't recognize sitting in the family parking lot behind the shop. I could see that someone was inside, but not much more than that. My pulse sped up as the car door opened just as I reached the back steps of Where There's Soap, and I had to fight the urge to run inside and dead bolt the door behind me before they could do something to me.

"Ben? Can I talk to you?"

It was Heather Kent from A Long Lost Soap, probably the last person in the world I expected to see that morning.

"Sure, come on inside. I'll fix us some coffee."

She looked at the shop—and the back stairs in particular—with obvious distaste. "Would it be possible for us to go somewhere else? I'm not really comfortable talking to you here. Do you mind?"

"That's fine," I said. "I know a place we can talk. I'll be with you in a minute. Just let me tell one of my brothers where I'm going to be in case they need me."

I slipped inside the door and found Bob staring at the equipment on the production line. "What's going on?" I asked him.

"The shifter's still not working properly. I know I made that part correctly, but I can't figure out what the problem is. We really have to change the layout of this line. It's driving me crazy the way it is."

I knew just enough about the situation to realize that his ideas were worth a lot more than mine on the topic. "Is there anything I can do to help?"

He shook his head. "I doubt it."

"Thanks for the vote of confidence."

Bob said, "I know you're the go-to guy around here, but this is out of your league."

I couldn't argue with that. Besides, I had something else to do at the moment. "Good enough. I'll see you later then."

"Don't go away mad," he said.

"I know, I know; just go away, right?"

Bob looked startled as I walked away. He called out, "Hey, Ben, I was just kidding. You don't have to go. You know how I get when I'm trying to fix a problem. My wife's surely given me enough grief about it over the years."

For him, it was a sterling apology, not that I needed it. I'd grown tough skin when it came to dealing with my family, and it would take more than a few cracks from Bob to get me going. "It's okay, really. I'd love to stick around, but I've got a breakfast date with a beautiful college coed. She's waiting right outside for me."

Bob said, "Yeah, right. You've been drinking that crazy tea Louisa's been pushing on all of us, haven't you?"

Just then, Heather tapped on the door, and I saw my brother's jaw drop. I said, "I'll be back as soon as I can."

"See you," was all he managed to say before I left.

I had to laugh, wondering what Bob might be thinking. I wasn't about to dissuade him of whatever notions he had.

I walked outside and joined Heather. "Sorry, I had to talk to my brother first. Are you ready?"

"Let's go. We can take my car."

"I've got a better idea. Why don't we walk over to The Hound Dog? They make better coffee than I do, anyway. We should be able to talk there."

I locked the door behind us, then we walked a block to The Hound Dog Café, a place that was stuck in a surreal Elvis Presley world. There were posters on the walls featuring The King in his movies, album covers under glass, and an area near the cash register that never failed to get a smile. Ruby Harlow, the owner of the café, had photographs ranging from the young Elvis all the way to the end when he was splitting his sequined jumpsuits. A jukebox stood in one corner, and heaven help the patron who asked why there were only Elvis tunes on it. There was a good-size crowd there already, and the place was buzzing with a dozen different conversations.

"Morning, Ruby," I said. "Could we have two coffees, please?" The café owner—a rail-thin woman in her fifties—sported a brunette bouffant hairdo that had gone out in the fifties, and her waitress's outfit was a replica made just for her, based on a character in one of Elvis's movies. I kept forgetting which one, and I was afraid to ask her again, lest she think I didn't care, which was the truth, but I wasn't about to hurt her feelings if I could help it. Besides, Elvis did kind of grow on me after a while.

Ruby winked at Heather, then said, "He's a big spender, isn't he? Go ahead, honey, order breakfast. Don't believe a word he tells you, I know for a fact that Ben here can afford it."

"Coffee's fine," Heather said, still not knowing what to make of the place. In the background, Ruby had one of her *Elvis's Greatest Hits* CDs going, but it was low enough for us to chat over the music.

Ruby slid the coffees in front of us, slipping the bill under my saucer before disappearing back up front. We'd chosen an empty table by one of the broad windows, and as I stirred the cream into my coffee, I watched as the world started waking up and passing us by.

Heather took a sip, then said, "Mmm, this is really good."

"Yeah, and you get all Elvis–all the time to boot."

Heather gestured around the room and asked, "Is this for show, or is she really that big a fan?"

I lowered my voice as I explained, "Ruby considers herself the world's biggest Elvis fan. She closes the café twice a year, a week each time. Guess where she goes?"

"Don't tell me: Graceland."

I didn't even try to contain my smile. "You got it on the

first try. She says there's nothing like Memphis at Christmas and in the springtime. Here's something kind of interesting. If you can sing an Elvis tune from start to finish, you get a free cup of coffee the first time you do it. She takes it all pretty seriously. Don't let it throw you, though. She's got a sweet disposition and a sharp brain under that bouffant hair."

Heather looked intrigued by the setup. "I'm just curious, but what do Elvis impersonators get? Does she like them, or does she shoot them on sight?"

It was a fair question. "You've got to be kidding. They eat on the house, at least the first time. Ruby's a fan, but she's still operating a business." I took another sip of coffee, then asked, "So what brings you here? I know you're looking for more than my company, no matter how pleasant you might find it. We didn't exactly get off on the right foot, did we?"

Her gaze shot down to her coffee. "I'm sorry about that. It's just that every time I've talked to you, I end up getting upset. Ben, we need to talk." She looked out the window a few seconds, then said, "The police came to see me again yesterday afternoon."

"I told you they probably would."

Heather said, "That woman—I think her name was Molly or Polly—kept staring at me like she didn't believe a word I said."

"It's Molly, and don't let it rattle you. She treats everybody like that. I honestly believe she thinks it's a part of her job."

"Well I didn't appreciate it. She made me feel guilty, and I haven't done anything wrong."

I shrugged. "Then you don't have anything to worry about."

"That's just it. There's something I should have told her, but she made me so nervous I couldn't bring myself to say it."

How had I suddenly been appointed as the go-between with Molly and the rest of the soapmaking world? "Heather, believe me, it will be better for you if you go to her with whatever you know. If she finds out from somebody else, Molly will chew away at you like a dog after a bone."

If she'd expected comfort from me, she wasn't going to get much. After all, Heather was still high on my list of suspects, no matter how nice she was being at the moment.

She said, "That's what I'm afraid of. Listen, Ben, I need a favor. If I tell you, will you tell her for me?"

I wanted to say no, I really did. Instead, I heard myself saying, "Absolutely. What's on your mind?"

My acquiescence was rewarded with her hesitation. "You know, maybe this wasn't such a good idea after all. I probably should just go."

She started to get up, and there was really no way I could stop her, but I had to at least try. "Heather, don't you think you'll feel better telling someone? If you don't, it's not going to give you any peace. I'm willing to listen, and I promise I won't judge you." I'd try not to, anyway.

She appeared to think about it for a few seconds, then finally said, "I can't. It's not right."

And then she was gone. I couldn't give up, though. I threw Ruby a five and said, "See you later."

Heather was halfway back to her car by the time I caught up with her. I was suddenly glad I'd kept my walking regimen up. "Hey, hang on a second."

She kept walking purposefully toward her car. "I can't, Ben. I'm sorry, I shouldn't have come to you. I made a mistake."

I took a deep breath, then said, "Why don't you tell me and let me decide for myself."

She hesitated, then stopped on the sidewalk and looked up at me. "It's about a rumor I heard, and I absolutely hate gossip. Ordinarily I'd just forget it, but this might be important."

"You can trust me."

Finally, she must have believed that I was sincere. "The only reason I'm coming to you is that it might help your sister. I may know who killed Jerry."

That got my full attention. "Tell me all about it."

She said, "I'm not even sure if what I overheard was true. You know what? I might as well tell you, this is ridiculous. I think John Labott might have had something to do with Jerry's death."

"John? Are you sure?" There was no way I could see John doing anything like that. He was the nicest, most level-headed guy I knew.

Heather seemed pretty sure, though. "It was John. There's no doubt in my mind."

"What exactly did you hear? Who was doing the talking?"

Heather said, "I'm not going to say, so don't ask me. I overheard something that wasn't meant for me to hear."

"At least tell me what they said," I pushed. "You can't leave it at this."

Heather bit her lower lip, then said, "Okay, I heard that the only way John was going to get to Louisa was by getting rid of his competition. It was said as a joke, but there was a ring of truth behind it. I like John, and I hate repeating something like this, but is there any chance it could be true?"

I suddenly felt better about her nervousness. "He likes Louisa, I know that much. Would he get rid of Jerry to get closer to her? I find that nearly impossible to believe."

"But do you think it's possible?"

I nodded. "I guess it could be, but John asked Louisa out long before Jerry started calling on us, and she turned him down flat. Are you sure you won't tell me where you heard this?"

She shook her head and started walking again. "I've said too much as it is. I've made such a fool out of myself."

"You did what you felt you had to. Heather, thanks for caring enough to come to me with this. I really do appreciate it." There were two ways I saw it. Heather could have been sincere in her desire to help, or she could be trying to divert suspicion to someone else. If she was sincere, the apology was heartfelt, but if she was trying to deceive me and I found out about it, it wouldn't sit lightly with me.

I managed to keep up with her all the way back to her car, but I couldn't get her to say another word.

As Heather drove away, Cindy popped her head out the back door. She said angrily, "I can't believe you're two-timing Kelly after one date. What is it with you men?"

It appeared that my baby sister was giving Mom a run for conclusion jumping. If it was an Olympic event, my family would be well represented on the team. "Has anybody in this family heard of personal privacy?"

Cindy said, "You're kidding, right? Now get in here, I want to hear what you think you're doing with that child when you're dating a perfectly nice woman closer to your own age."

I nearly got in the Miata and drove off to avoid the grilling I was going to get, but I knew ultimately it would just delay the inquisition.

As I walked past my little sister into the soap shop, I said, "Before you get all wound up, that was Heather Kent. She's running A Long Lost Soap while her grandparents are on a cruise."

"And you're dating her, too? Isn't one woman enough for you all of a sudden?"

Trying to keep from yelling, I said, "I'm not dating Heather Kent. She wanted to talk to me about something, so we had coffee at The Hound Dog. There's nothing more to it than that."

Cindy appeared to buy it, but just barely. "What was so important, anyway?"

"It was about Jerry Sanger's murder," I said. "I'm still working on it, you know."

Cindy softened at once. "I know you are, Ben; I didn't mean to push. I just didn't want to see you do something stupid and jeopardize your relationship with Kelly."

"Cindy, you're my sister and I love you, but you need to butt out of my life. Pass that on to Kate and Mom for me, too, would you?"

If she was offended by my blunt comments, she didn't show it. "We love you, you big goofball. That's why we want you to be happy."

"I'm happy enough," I said.

"Yes, but you could be happier, I just know it. So how was your date?"

"It was fine," I said. I knew there was no way she was going to accept that answer, but I wasn't in a sharing mood.

"It was more than that; I see that gleam in your eye. Are you seeing her again?"

I reluctantly admitted, "If you must know, we're going out tonight."

Cindy all but squealed with delight. "I knew it; I just knew you two would hit it off if you ever had a chance. Where are you taking her?"

My decision the night before sounded kind of foolish in the cold light of morning. I admitted, "Actually, she's coming over to my apartment. I'm cooking dinner for her."

When Cindy saw that I wasn't kidding, she exploded. "You're what? Ben, are you out of your mind? You could burn water; I've seen it. What makes you think you can cook an entire meal?"

"Hey, I've been practicing. I'm getting pretty good at it, if I say so myself."

Cindy ignored me and said, "Here's what we'll do. Kate can make the main course, I'll bake a cake for dessert, and Louisa can handle the salad. We can have it at your apartment before Kelly gets there. Hey, you can even take credit for the meal if you want to."

I took my sister's shoulders in my hands and said, "Cindy, listen to me. I'm the oldest kid in this zoo we call a family. I'm doing this on my own, with no help from any of you ladies, no matter how well meaning it is."

She shrugged when she saw that I wasn't going to budge. "Well, you can't say I didn't try. If you're determined to wreck this on your own, there's nothing any of us can do about it."

"Thanks for your unbridled optimism. Now if you'll excuse me, I've got some work to do."

I went upstairs to my office, trying to wade through the paperwork collecting on my desk, but my thoughts kept drifting back to Jerry Sanger's murder. The man had certainly generated enough enemies to last a lifetime. How could someone make that many folks mad at him at one time? He'd generated his share of dislike, but which of the suspects on my list hated him enough to kill him? I wasn't any closer to answering it when there was a knock on my door.

"Come in."

My brother Bob poked his head in. "Listen, I hate to bother you, but I just wanted to say I was sorry."

The past few days had been filled with firsts, but that might have been the most surprising. "Apology accepted. Now what exactly are you apologizing for?"

"For doubting you before. I just wanted to ask you something. Don't you think you're a little old to be dating a teenager?"

"She's not a teenager, we're not dating, and I'm not that

old. Some women prefer a mature man." It felt like my family was absolutely going out of their way to drive me crazy.

Bob looked uncertain, then said, "So you're not dating her, I get it. Does that mean you're not going out with Kelly Sheer, either?"

I threw my hands into the air. "You caught me. That one I'll admit to."

Bob appeared to ponder that for a minute, then said, "What's Molly think about all that? Or does she know?"

I'd had enough of my siblings and their prying. "Bob, Molly and I have an agreement. We date whoever we choose to."

"But does she know?" he asked stubbornly.

"She saw us together last night. We talked about it. It's cool. She knows."

Bob said, "You should treat her better than that. She deserves it."

"I haven't done anything wrong," I said.

"She deserves better," he repeated.

"Then tell Jeff to ask her out and stop pining away for her," I said, fully tired of that particular conversation.

"I might do just that."

"Be my guest. There's just one thing, though."

"What's that?" Bob asked.

"I don't want to hear about it, one way or the other. It's really none of my business. Let's keep it that way, okay?"

"It's a deal."

After he left, I wondered what I really thought about the prospect of my youngest brother dating my onetime and sometime girlfriend. A part of me had wanted to object, but what sense did that make? The agreement that freed me to date Kelly had to work both ways. I wasn't sure how easily I'd handle it if Molly and Jeff hit it off and started dating, but I figured I'd burn that bridge when I came to it. For the moment, I needed to talk to John Labott and see how much truth there might be to the rumor that he might have had something to do with Jerry Sanger's death, no matter how remote the possibility seemed to me.

TEN

○ ○ ○

I called John's office to track him down and was surprised to discover that Where There's Soap was already on his calling schedule for later in the day. It was beginning to look like my suspects were all going to come to me. Great, just when I wanted an excuse to get away from my family, it appeared that I was going be at the shop all day. I waded through some of the paperwork on my desk, worked on the line for ten minutes with my brothers—despite their protests—and then helped Louisa with her monthly inventory. I hadn't hung around with the guys very long; Bob was acting odder than usual, no doubt because of our earlier conversation.

The brightest part of my morning was a call from Kelly just before lunch.

The second I heard her voice, I said, "You're not bailing out on me, are you?"

"Not on your life. I just forgot to ask if there was anything I could bring tonight."

"No, I've got it covered. I'm really looking forward to having dinner with you again."

"Me too," she said. "I'll see you tonight."

"Bye," I said. I'd made a grocery list of all of the ingredients for the meal I'd be buying on the way home, and I pulled it out again to make sure I hadn't forgotten anything. I had half expected John to come by Where There's Soap in the morning, but he still wasn't there by noon. I was hungry, but I didn't want to leave the shop and take a chance on missing him. Kate found me in my office and said, "Come on, we're ready to eat."

"What are you talking about?"

"Did Mom forget to tell you, too? She's instituting a new company policy. One day a week all employees will eat in the break room together. Today's the day."

My mother was notorious for instituting policy changes without a moment's notice, but I had a suspicion there was something at work here besides one of her capricious whims. "All employees meaning all of the family. She's going to keep us together if it kills her, isn't she? I suppose Grandpa is here, too."

"Ben, you really are out of the loop. He left for England this morning. You're doing the advertising while he's gone. Don't you and Mom ever talk?"

"I've been busy," I said.

She tapped one of the piles of paper on my desk. "Well, it's all in the memo. Now hurry up—we're waiting for you."

I followed her downstairs and asked, "So who's minding the shop while we eat? I can't imagine Mom shutting the place down."

My sister shook her head. "If you'd read the memo, you'd know we're on a rotating schedule. One of us watches the counter and eats later." She grinned. "Even you boys have to take your turn waiting on customers."

I could just see my brothers working the front. Mom must have really been desperate for some family time to allow that. "I'm not sure that's all that great an idea. I've handled the front before, but the other guys aren't exactly customer-friendly."

She grinned mischievously. "I know; I can't wait. Maybe then they'll stop complaining about how they do all the real work around here. It wouldn't surprise me if that was Mom's plan all along."

"No, it wouldn't surprise me, either. So who pulled the cash register duty today?"

Kate said, "Louisa. She says she doesn't mind being left out a bit."

"I wonder if she'd trade places with me."

Kate smacked my arm lightly. "Ben, you're terrible. Come on, it won't be that bad."

"I can't imagine how you could possibly think that. Just wait."

Everybody was already in the break room when Kate and I arrived. Most of their plates were filled, and Mom had dragged in enough chairs so all of us could sit as we ate. Kate and I grabbed some plates and hit the buffet line, and I had to admit, it was kind of fun being together like that. I should have known there was more to my mother's act than a mini family reunion, though. After we ate the fried chicken and fixings Mom had made for us, she closed the door and turned to me. "Ben, can you give us a progress report on the murder investigation?"

I nodded. The reason behind the new company policy had suddenly become clear. "So that's why we're in here and Louisa's out there. I have to hand it to you, Mom, you're good."

My mother said huffily, "I don't know what you're talking about. That's just the way the schedule happened to work out this week."

I couldn't contain my grin. "And you're the one who made the schedule. I give up, I've been played by a master. Okay, here's where we stand. There are several suspects. They all had one reason or another for wanting to wish ill of our late supplier, but did any of them hate him enough to kill him? Obviously one of them did, since that's what happened, but I haven't figured out yet exactly which one did it."

"So who are we considering?" Mom asked.

I ticked them off on my fingers. "Let's see, so far I've come up with Monique White, Heather Kent, Steve Erickson, Melissa Higgins, John Labott, and all of you."

Mom said, "Benjamin, that's not funny."

I put my plate down. "It wasn't meant to be. Mom, you can't tell me any of us wouldn't have done something to protect Louisa if we thought we had to, including you."

"So you suspect all of us?" Jim asked, not surprised at all by my statement.

"Of course not, you nit. I'm just saying, we all had reason to wish ill of that man."

He looked disappointed by my admission, causing me to wonder yet again about one of my siblings. At times they could all be mad as hatters.

Kate said, "You can't honestly think Melissa Higgins had anything to do with Jerry's murder. And John Labott? He wouldn't step on an ant."

"Someone thinks he could do a great deal more than that. He's coming by today, so I'm going to ask him myself."

"Has anything else happened?" Mom asked.

I stood and said, "That's right, I forgot you all don't know about the telephone message I got last night." I relayed it to them, along with my belief that one of the folks I'd been talking to had felt the urge to threaten me.

"So where does that leave you?" Kate asked.

"Like I said, I want to talk to John to see if there's any truth to the rumor I heard about him. Molly's got her people looking at the tape, but I've got a feeling that's going to be a dead end. The voice was disguised pretty well. Other than that, I'm going to keep digging and see what rocks I can turn over."

Louisa came in just then and said, "Can someone relieve me? I'm starving and I can smell that chicken in the shop. Hey, I didn't know we were having a family meeting, too."

"We're just chatting," Mom said levelly. "Kate, take the floor so your sister can eat."

Louisa said, "She can deal with John Labott, too."

"John's here?" I asked. "I need to speak with him."

"Help yourself. He's constantly looking at me like he wants to say something, but he never manages more than hello and good-bye. It's driving me nuts."

I walked out with Kate, and while she waited on the single customer in the shop, I pulled John aside. "Hi, John, do you have a minute?"

His smile was warm and open. "All the time you need. Like I said before, I've got some great new molds to show you today."

"Good." I started walking toward the back door, and John asked, "Aren't we going to your office?"

I'd originally planned on exactly that, but I'd suddenly come up with another idea. "It's such a pretty day I thought we'd talk outside." I needed to get him on the back steps where Jerry Sanger had been murdered, since I wanted him off balance for the questions I was going to be asking.

As we walked through the production line, I said, "I hear you two didn't care for each other."

He looked at me oddly as we moved to the back steps. "What are you talking about, Ben?"

"I mean Jerry Sanger. He was killed right there where you're standing, you know."

John avoided my look. "I hadn't heard where it was, just that it was somewhere around the shop."

"I found him right where you're standing," I said, though in truth he was off by a couple of steps.

John hurried off the steps and stood on the concrete landing below. "Have you been drinking or something? I don't understand why you're acting like this, Ben. I thought we were friends. This is getting too weird for me."

I hated doing it, but I had to keep reminding myself that I was looking for a murderer. If I bruised a few feelings on the way, I'd find a way to make up for it down the road. "How do you think we feel, having someone murdered on our back steps? We don't appreciate it, and we're going to find out who did it, whether the police manage to or not. So tell me, is it true you wanted him out of the way so you'd have a shot at my sister?"

"I can't believe you're even thinking that, let alone saying it out loud."

I stepped closer to him. "But is it true?"

He backed up and hit against the loading dock. "Of course not."

"Then why did someone tell me this morning that the reason you hated Sanger was because he was dating Louisa?"

Now John was getting mad, I could see it in his eyes. "Dating? You call that dating? He was using her, and whether you know it or not, your sister deserves better treatment than that."

"And now that your competition's gone, you're willing to be the one to supply it, is that it?"

John looked fiercely at me and said, "What's gotten into you, Ben? You're not like this."

"I am when it comes to defending my family. I need to

know, for my sake as well as my sister's. I'm going to ask you one last time. Did you have anything to do with Jerry Sanger's murder?"

"No, I didn't," John said, spitting out the words. "I'm going."

"What about your sales pitch?"

He frowned, then said, "It can wait until someone else is free. I'm not much in the mood to deal with you right now." He walked away with his fists clinched, and for a second, just before he left, I thought he might take a swing at me.

If his indignation was feigned, he was doing an excellent job of it. Or was the reaction I'd seen just from being named a suspect? He had reason to dislike Jerry Sanger if he was jealous of the man's relationship with my sister, but did he have motive enough to kill him? And if he had dispatched his rival, why hadn't he made any effort to ask Louisa out now that the field was clear? There was certainly no reason for him to wait, not if he'd committed the murder to be with her. I wasn't ready to take John Labott off my list of suspects, but he wasn't in the top three. I left those slots open for Monique White, Heather Kent, and Steve Erickson. In John's tier of suspects, I included Melissa Higgins and the rest of my family, including Louisa. They were all possible, but not that probable, in my book. I didn't see any of them killing the salesman, but members of my family aren't strangers to rash behavior, and it was possible, whether I wanted to admit it or not.

I walked back into Where There's Soap, and Kate asked, "Where's John?"

"He had to go," I said.

"He left out the back way without at least trying to talk to Louisa first? What did you say to him, Ben?"

I wasn't about to admit that I'd just browbeaten the man. "I didn't say anything. He just didn't have any more time for us."

"Ben," Kate said, tapping her heel on the hardwood floor.

So denial wasn't going to work. "Okay, I may have said something to him about Jerry Sanger's murder."

"Benjamin Perkins, do you honestly think that man has it in him to kill someone?"

I held my hands out, palms upward. "I don't know, Kate, that's why I'm asking so many questions. Just be glad I haven't focused on the family yet."

That certainly got her attention. "What do you mean by that? Were you actually serious earlier?" I regretted the comment as soon as I'd said it, but there was no backing down with Kate once I had. In a steady voice, I said, "We're all overprotective of the family. Can you honestly say that if you thought someone outside the family was destroying one of us, you wouldn't take steps to correct it?"

She looked shocked by the very idea of it. "I'd try to protect someone I loved, but murder? Do you think any of us is capable of it?"

"Kate, I'm not accusing anybody of anything. But somebody killed Jerry Sanger; he didn't splash that lye on himself and then throw himself down the back steps."

"You know what? I'm not at all sure I want to talk to you right now either," she said.

"Join the club: the line forms at the rear."

Kate said stiffly, "Maybe you should work with Bob and Jim and Jeff for the rest of the day."

I didn't expect a lot of thanks for what I was doing, but I wasn't going to take abuse for trying to get my sister off, either. "Don't worry, I'll teach my class and then I'll get out of here."

Kate said, "Ben, I didn't mean . . . wait . . ."

I wasn't in the mood for apologies. "Sorry, I've got to get ready for my class, but if you'd like, I'll schedule you for another lambasting session when I'm finished. In the meantime, I'm going to see what I can do to get our sister off the hook."

I shouldn't have been so abrupt with Kate—I knew she was just trying to help—and I'd known since she was three days old that she was more sensitive than the rest of the Perkins kids. She cried at long-distance telephone commercials; why in the world hadn't I considered that and kept my mouth shut? Then I had compounded the mistake by walking out on her and not giving her the chance to make peace. Sometimes I acted like the baby of the family, even though chronologically I was the oldest. I decided that after my class, I'd have to find a way to apologize to Kate and make things right, but at the moment, I wasn't in the mood to be around anybody in my family.

I waited as long as I could to start my class, hoping that Herbert and Constance would show up at the last minute, but three minutes after class was due to start, they were still missing. I spoke to the group gathered there. "Now that we've mastered the basics of melt-and-pour soapmaking, let's have a little fun with the process." I passed some of my samples of variegated, swirled, layered, and special scented soaps around as I explained, "Don't let the complicated appearance of these pieces fool you. I made every one of these samples using melt-and-pour techniques. If everyone will gather around the worktable here, I'll give you a quick lesson and then you can try your own hand at it."

The session passed by quickly enough, but my heart wasn't in it. I couldn't tell if it was because of the absence of my two most animated pupils or the weight of the murder investigation on my mind, but it was all I could do to keep my mind on teaching the class. My pupils could tell it, too, and instead of a fun experience, there were a few strained laughs and a great deal more silence than I was used to. As they left the shop with their creations, Cindy said, "You got a call from the hospital while you were teaching."

"What's Monique want now?" I asked.

She shook her head and handed me the note. "It's not Monique. A woman from your class named Constance called. She said she was sorry they missed today's session, but someone named Herbert had a heart attack. She said you'd know who she was."

So that was why my star pupils had been absent. "Did she say had bad it was?"

"No, just that she was at the hospital with him."

I grabbed my jacket. I'd planned to go see Monique again, so I might as well drop in on Constance and Herbert at the same time. "I'm going to the hospital," I said.

Cindy looked surprised by my reaction. "Wow, you really get close to your students, don't you?"

"That's part of teaching," I said and headed for the door.

I stopped by the cardiac ICU as soon as I got to the hospital. I found Constance in the waiting room, carefully watching the nurse's station. She didn't see me until I was standing over her. "Hi, Constance; how's he doing?"

She looked happy to see me, but she was obviously surprised by my presence. "Ben? You didn't have to come by. That's not why I called. I just didn't want you to worry about us when we didn't show up."

I sat down beside her. "I had to visit a sick friend anyway, so I thought I'd stop by here first. Is it bad?"

She tilted her head, then said, "To hear him tell it, he didn't have a heart attack at all; he keeps claiming he just had a gas episode from too much spicy food; the old fool. It was all I could do to get him to come here in the first place."

"What have the doctors said?"

She kept twisting a white linen handkerchief with her fingers as she spoke. "It was a mild heart attack, but he's got to make some changes, including more exercise and less fatty foods. He doesn't believe them, of course."

The poor woman was going to have her hands full. If Herbert was grumpy when he was perfectly healthy, I couldn't imagine how he was behaving under this kind of stress. "Are you going to be okay?"

She smiled. "I will. Thanks for asking. You know, the main reason I'm worried right now is that he's being so polite to everyone. It's hard to take, and absolutely out of character for him."

"Chances are he's just scared."

She nodded. "Who wouldn't be, but get him to admit it. I'd like it a lot better if he was giving folks around here more grief."

One of the ICU nurses approached us and said, "Mrs. Wilson, he's asking for you."

She looked worried as she asked, "How is he?"

"Well, I can't say much for his disposition, but his vital signs are all good."

That brought a broad smile to Constance's face. "Thank goodness for that."

She nodded. "You got him here in plenty of time. His signs are really strong."

"You don't understand. His attitude is a better barometer than a readout on a monitor, trust me. If he's snippy, that means he's feeling better."

The nurse let a slight smile slip out. "Then he must be feeling dandy at the moment."

Constance and I stood, then she hugged me. "Thanks for coming, Ben."

"You're very welcome. Tell Herbert I said hello."

"I will."

As I walked to Monique's room, I marveled at how

close Constance and Herbert were, despite their constant public debates. Folks always seemed to find their own way, and contrary to the way they acted, the underlying love was readily apparent between them.

Monique's bed was empty, the room devoid of the floral exhibition that had been there earlier. I found a new nurse at the station and asked about her.

"She left ten minutes ago," the woman said with obvious relief.

"Did she say if she was going home?" I asked.

As the nurse glanced over some paperwork, she said, "She didn't say, but she kept fussing that she needed to get out of here. We told her she needed bed rest. I personally don't think we should have discharged her."

"Why's that?"

The nurse shrugged. "She said she was going to a soap bubble. Now I ask you, is that a rational thing to say? Obviously she's still feeling the effects of that blow to the head."

I didn't correct her as I raced out the door. Let her wonder. What could be so pressing at her soap shop that Monique felt forced to go there just after checking out of the hospital? She hadn't had much of a head start, and if I was lucky I might be able to catch her before she had the chance to act. Whatever she was up to, I was certain it meant something.

I found Monique's car in front of her shop, but the CLOSED sign was still in place. I'd hoped to catch her off guard. Testing the door, I was surprised to find that it wasn't locked, though it had been repaired since the assault. Instead of calling her name, I walked carefully through the doorway. At the last second I remembered the bell on the door and gently eased it out of the way as I shut it behind me. There were noises in back of the shop in the same area where I'd found her before.

Creeping to the edge of the doorway, I looked inside and saw Monique on a ladder fiddling with something in the attic. I was still deciding if I wanted to say something or not when I accidentally nudged a display, sending a stack of beauty bars crashing to the floor.

When I looked up at Monique, I found myself staring down the barrel of a gun.

ELEVEN

o o o

"TAKE it easy," I said, holding my hands up. "It's just me."

The look of relief on Monique's face was obvious. "Oh for goodness's sake, Ben, you nearly gave me a heart attack."

"You mean like the one you're giving me right now? Do you mind pointing that somewhere else?"

She said, "Oh, sorry, of course." As she lowered the gun, I asked, "What are you doing up on a ladder, anyway?"

She climbed down and put the handgun on the counter. "I thought I heard squirrels in the attic again."

"So you were going to shoot them?" I asked.

"No, that would be nonsense. Chances are all I'd manage to do would be to shoot up the roof."

"So why the gun?" I asked.

She frowned. "I'm a woman working alone here. I've been assaulted once, and I'm not willing to take any more chances. I don't have a big family looking out for me. I'm all alone."

I gestured to the handgun on the counter. "Monique, do you even have a permit for that thing?"

She shook her head. "It was my father's; he left it to me in his will. It was practically all I got from him, but at least it still works. I suppose it does, at any rate."

"I don't know how wise it is for you to go around your shop armed."

Monique said, "Ben, I appreciate you worrying about me, but it makes me feel better having it. Besides, I don't exactly tote it around in my purse. It's usually under the counter."

I decided to change the subject. "You're back to work awfully soon, aren't you?"

She misinterpreted my intent. "It's so sweet of you to worry, but I'll be fine. A girl's got to have something to do, doesn't she?" Monique faltered slightly, then said, "Ben, I'll tell you the truth. I was afraid that if I didn't come straight back here from the hospital, I'd never be able to come back at all. It's important to take away the bad memory and replace it with something good. I wanted to be among my things again."

"I guess I understand that."

Monique said, "But how did you get in? I didn't even hear the bell."

There was a very good reason for that, but I wasn't about to enlighten her. "Your head must have been in the attic. I'd advise you to be more careful in the future. The front door wasn't locked."

"I slipped up. It won't happen again." She patted the gun as she said, "Believe me, I'll be careful. Now if you'll excuse me, I've got to get things ready for my reopening."

I knew arguing with her would be useless, but I couldn't just leave her there. "Is there anything I can do to help?"

She frowned at the display case, still askew from when it had struck her. "I hate to ask, but could you nudge that back in place for me? It's giving me the creeps just looking at it."

"I'd be glad to." The cherrywood was heavy, but I managed to move it back without too much difficulty. "How's that?" I asked.

"Much better."

I started to put the stock back on the shelf, but she said, "Honestly, I can do that."

"I don't mind," I said.

She took a bar of luffa soap out of my hands and said, "Ben, I appreciate it, but it's going to take me longer to straighten out your help than it will to do it myself."

I agreed reluctantly. She was hiding something, but I couldn't for the life of me figure out what it was. Since her accident, Monique was acting even odder than usual. I took the ladder and closed it. "At least let me put this away. Where does it go?"

"Thank you, it is rather heavy. It goes back here. Come on, I'll show you where."

After I had the ladder stowed back in the storage room, I said, "Well, I won't keep you."

"I'm curious, how did you know I'd be here?" she asked.

"I stopped by the hospital to check on you, but they told me you'd already checked out."

That seemed to mollify her. "I'm as fit as a fiddle. Thank you again for your concern. Now I'm sure your family needs you back at Where There's Soap."

"I'll come by tomorrow to look in on you," I said. I was still not satisfied with Monique's behavior, and I wanted to get close enough to ask her about Jerry Sanger without raising her suspicions.

"Until then," she said as she walked me out the door.

My foot was just on the front stoop when I heard the dead bolt click in place behind me. She might be getting ready to open again, but it didn't appear that she'd be doing it any time soon. I decided to circle around the building to see what she was up to once she thought I was gone.

I had a hard time spotting her without being seen, but I finally found her in back, talking heatedly on the telephone. I wasn't close enough to hear any specific words, but I could tell she was extremely agitated about something. After Monique hung up, I saw her take one of the gift baskets she stocked and throw it across the room. Whatever had happened, Monique hadn't been thrilled with the outcome. I kept waiting for her to do something else. Finally, I saw her disappear into her office, and if I held my head just right, I could see her sitting at her desk.

She must have seen me, too! I saw her get up in a hurry, so I raced back to my Miata. I just had my key in the ignition when she burst out the front door.

"Why are you still here?"

I thought of the only lie I could on the spot. "I'm having trouble with my car. It won't start." I was trying to catch my breath from my sprint and not give Monique any indication that I'd been spying on her.

"Do you want me to call a tow truck?"

"No, let me try something first." I popped the hood, stared inside at the incomprehensible array of hoses, belts, and cables, pretended to wiggle a couple just enough to get my hands dirty, then slammed the hood shut.

"That should do it," I said confidently. I was just hoping I hadn't disabled it by accident in my ruse to fix it. What I knew about cars could fit in a thimble with room left over.

Thankfully the Miata started right up. Monique said, "You're a real Renaissance man, aren't you?"

"Hey, I try," I said, then drove off. I noticed that

Monique was still watching me as I turned the corner, and I wondered if my mechanic's impression had fooled her.

At least she hadn't come outside with the gun in her hand.

I glanced at my watch and realized that I didn't have time to go back to Where There's Soap after all. Kelly was coming to the apartment for dinner, and I had a thousand things to do before she got there. First on the list was grocery shopping on the way home. Then, while I had dinner cooking, I was going to have to do a major cleaning job on my apartment. There would be time later, if we kept going out, to reveal my less than perfect housekeeping skills. For now, I was still doing everything possible to make the best impression I could.

I didn't know what my sisters were worried about. I had everything under control for my dinner with Kelly. The barbequed chicken breasts were in the oven, the apartment was the cleanest it had been in years, and I was ready to take a quick shower to get ready for my date. I'd originally gotten the recipe for the chicken off a bottle of barbeque sauce, and I'd had some luck with it before. It was easy, nearly foolproof, and didn't require much prep work at all; in other words, my perfect meal.

I thought I heard something as the shower ran, but it wasn't until I cut the water off to shampoo my hair that I heard what it was. The smoke alarm was blaring out in full voice.

Blast it all! I grabbed my robe and threw it on, the shampoo suds dripping down my face. In the kitchen, there was ominous black smoke coming from the oven. That's when I remembered I'd forgotten to set the timer. I threw open the oven door, and instead of finding the golden chicken breasts I'd expected, there was a distinct black crust over everything.

I threw a window open to try to dissipate some of the fumes, and then I got to work on the smoke detector. The blasted button wouldn't deactivate, so I finally had to pull a chair over to it and jerk the battery out.

That's when I heard the doorbell.

Saying a silent prayer that Kelly wasn't early, I looked out the peephole and found her waiting by my front door.

The second I opened it, she took the scene in and said, "I'm early. I'm so sorry. I'll come back."

If she gave me three hours it wouldn't improve the situation. "It's not going to get much better than this. If you're feeling adventurous, you might as well come in."

She smiled. "It can't be as bad as all that, can it?"

"You'd be surprised. Seriously, if you'd like to take a rain check, we can do this again some other time."

Kelly said, "Ben, I'm not some glass princess. So this didn't work out. We can do something else. Tell you what, why don't you finish your shower and get dressed while I tidy up the kitchen? Go on, it's fine."

"You, my dear, are a saint."

I finished my shower and dressed quickly, happy that Kelly hadn't bailed out on me when she had every reason to. By the time I came back into the kitchen, she had it sparkling.

"So, was any of the bird salvageable?"

She shook her head. "I'm afraid not. That's fine, though, we can do something else for dinner."

"Well, I'd like to offer you something here, but all I've got is chocolate cake for dessert."

I heard a gentle chuckle. "What's wrong?"

"I guess I should have told you. I'm allergic to chocolate."

"This just keeps getting better and better, doesn't it?"

She took my hand and said, "It's not going to ruin the evening unless we let it. I've got an idea, if you're game for it."

I spread my hands. "Hey, we can both see what a great job I did planning tonight. What did you have in mind?"

"Why don't we have a picnic?"

It was a balmy evening—the cold front the night before had quickly passed us by—and my original plan hadn't worked out. "Why not?" I asked.

Louisa had given me a picnic hamper kit for Christmas one year, but I hadn't even taken it out of the cellophane wrapping. There were plates, silverware, wine glasses, and a corkscrew tucked inside, and I grabbed a bottle of wine from the rack.

"How's this?"

She looked impressed. "My, aren't you prepared."

"One of my sisters gave it to me as a present," I admitted.

"You all still exchange gifts? The Christmas tree must be ready to topple over from all the bounty underneath it."

I shook my head. "We exchange names now. That way we all don't go broke buying things for everyone else." As we walked outside, I said, "Would you like to take the Miata again?"

Kelly smiled. "You drove last night, so why don't we take my car tonight?"

"That sounds good. I've never ridden in a Mercedes before."

She said, "It was a gift, too."

"Wow, I hope I don't draw your name at Christmas," I said as I slid onto the leather seat. "That's a tough act to follow."

She laughed, and I found myself wanting to amuse her just to hear the sound of it again. "I gave it to myself when I moved to Harper's Landing. It probably sounds silly, but it was kind of a single-again present."

"Has it been tough adjusting to so many changes in your life?" I asked.

As she drove, Kelly said, "It was at first. I hate to admit it, but Annie's had a lot easier time adapting to our new life than I have."

I nodded. "That's only natural. You left an entire history in Charlotte."

"Yes, but I'm finding advantages to living here, too."

We went by Max's Deli, though the owner's name was Stella and there had never been a Max in the business as far as I knew, and we got all the makings for sandwiches. When we were set, I said, "I guess the only question is where we should have this impromptu dinner party of ours."

Kelly appeared to think about it for a few seconds, then asked, "Could we go to the dam? I've heard it's beautiful, but I haven't found anyone to take me there."

Remembering Louisa's recent brush with disaster, I said, "We could go there, but with all the rain we've been having lately, it's a muddy mess." Suddenly I knew just where I wanted to take her. "I know a place that won't be nearly as crowded, and it's a lot more pleasant."

"Then by all means, lead on."

I directed her to Leah's garden and told her to park by the entrance.

She grabbed the food supplies as I retrieved the basket and wine.

Kelly looked around at the iron fence and the close, overgrown trees. "Well, I understand why it's deserted here."

"Come on, have a little faith in me."

I offered my hand and she took it as we walked around the imposing iron-gated fence that appeared to surround the property. Kelly kept trying to look beyond the fence and the dense branches of the evergreens. "What is it, a cemetery?" She asked.

"Yes, I often invite my dates to dine among the tomb-stones with me." When she didn't respond, I said, "Hey, I'm kidding. We're nearly there."

I punched in the simple code that never changed on the back lock, and the mechanism released. I opened the gate and held it for Kelly.

"Go on in, it's okay," I said.

As she walked through, I hit the timer beside the gate, bringing the area to light for the maximum two hours of visitation allowed to a trusted few. Inside the enclosure and hidden from the world's view was the most marvelous garden in four states. The perimeter had been planted in hem-lock trees shoulder to shoulder in order to block out passersby, but inside were paths and benches sprinkled among the plantings of roses, annuals, and perennials, each more glorious than the patch before it, and a luxuriant lawn that would have shamed many of the golf courses in our area. The flower beds, all carefully carved from the lush green of the lawn, were backlit. In the center of the mosaic was a jetting fountain that danced with changing colorful lights and spurts of fire defying nature. In a small way, it reminded me of our herb garden in front of the soap shop, but there was no comparing the elegance or the scale of them. There was a simple granite table and bench positioned nearby to enjoy the view, and I guided Kelly to-ward them.

"What is this place?" Kelly asked, her voice soft in hushed wonder.

"It's beautiful, isn't it? In a way you were right. It's not a cemetery, but it is a memorial. Bartholomew Grant had this place created as a wedding present for his wife fifty years ago, and he's been improving it ever since."

She said, "What a wondrous gift. I bet they come here all the time. She must feel so lucky."

"Leah loved it, until she passed away two winters ago. It

looked like the flu, and she was starting to get over it when another nastier bug bit her. At first Bartholomew was lost without her, but he's found some measure of solace working on this place every spare moment he's got. Only a chosen few in all of Harper's Landing know it's even here, and even fewer are allowed inside."

"And how did you merit the privilege?" she asked.

"We've been friends for as long as I can remember. So what do you think?"

"It's unbelievable." Her shining eyes turned to me. "Thank you for sharing it with me. Tell the truth—you burned that chicken on purpose."

"I wish I could take the credit for it, but that was just fate at work. Are you ready to eat?"

"Absolutely."

I set our places at the table, and we had a wonderful meal under the stars. The day had been warm, and the evening was following suit. I glanced at my watch and was surprised to see that we had only a few minutes left on the timer. "I hate to break this up, but we need to go."

"Must we? I could stay here all night."

"I know exactly how you feel. We can come back another time, but Bartholomew allows only two hours a night. I hope you're not too disappointed."

"Not if you promise to bring me back sometime."

"That's a date," I said.

As we walked out the back gate, Kelly asked, "Aren't you going to turn out the lights?"

"Hang on a second." I glanced at the digital timer and saw it was nearly ready to go off. I took a deep breath, heard the click of power being cut, and blew toward the lights with all my strength. They died just as I finished.

She laughed heartily. "My goodness, you really pull out all the stops in order to impress a gal, don't you?"

"What can I say? I am a born romantic."

We walked back to the car, and and when we were
buckled in Kelly started to drive away. "So, where do you
want to go now?"

"I feel like I owe you dessert after the chocolate cake
disaster."

She said, "Tell you what, since you took care of dinner,
how about if I treat for dessert?"

"That sounds great. What did you have in mind?"

"Now it's your turn to trust me." She drove out of town,
and I was surprised when I saw that she was headed for
Fiddler's Grove. "Hey, just where are we going?"

She glanced over at me and asked, "You don't have to
be home early, do you? I thought a drive might be fun."

I admitted, "I've got all time in the world."

"Then let's enjoy the night."

We chatted quite a bit as we drove, and the time flew
past when she pulled up in front of a place called Kran-
kle's Bakery in a part of Fiddler's Grove I hadn't visited
before.

"Wow, they should really do something about their
name," I said as I got out. "It's not very appetizing, is it?"

She looked over at me and said, "Hey, be nice. That's
my maiden name."

"Oh, Kelly, I'm so sorry. I didn't mean anything by it."

She smiled. "Stop squirming, I was just kidding."

"Whew, for a second there I thought I was going to be
walking home."

"Come on, let's go in." We walked into the bakery and I
was overwhelmed with the most delightful combination of
aromas. There were rows of doughnuts, crullers, crois-
sants, loaves of exotic breads, and several confections I'd
never seen before. "So this is what heaven smells like," I
said aloud.

A large man with a nearly bald head and a shiny red
nose said, "If there's any justice in this world or the next, it

will to me. Welcome." He winked at Kelly and said, "And where's your little one tonight?"

"She's with her father, Gustav. This is my friend Ben."

He reached a meaty paw over the counter, and I shook it. "Pleased to meet you, Ben."

"Thanks, it's good meeting you." I gestured to the array of samples. "I can't imagine making a choice with all these options."

Kelly asked, "Do you trust me to choose, Ben?"

"Are you kidding? I'm counting on you to save me," I said.

Kelly smiled, then turned back to the baker. "Do you have apple crisps by any chance?"

"Would I keep my doors open if I didn't? Let me get you a couple." As he selected and wrapped two good-sized pieces of the feathery apple confection, I asked, "Don't most bakeries close by six?"

He said, "And more's the pity, in my opinion. The truth is, I've got insomnia, and my wife, she can't stay awake past seven in the evening, so we've worked it out this way. I bake in the morning with her, take a nap while she sells in the afternoon, then I stay open in the evenings."

"You don't get to spend much time together that way, do you? I'm sorry—that's really none of my business."

Gustav laughed heartily. "Oh, we close down completely two months of every year, and by the time our vacation is over, Hetta can't wait for our old hours. Everybody's happy that way, my friend."

Kelly accepted the pastries and slid her money across the counter. "Bye, Gustav."

"Good-bye, and enjoy. It was nice meeting you, Ben. Come back anytime."

"You can count on that," I said as I held the front door open for Kelly. I was pleased to see that she was appreciative of the gesture. I'd been scolded by women before for doing it, none more severe than Molly.

Kelly said, "Should we eat this in the car, or wait until we get back into town?"

"Let's wait. Truthfully, I'm still full from dinner."

As we drove back toward Harper's Landing, I asked, "How in the world did you ever find that place?"

As she drove, she explained, "Annie and I love to explore. We pick a different city nearby one weekend a month and spend a Saturday there. It's amazing the things you can discover that way."

"That sounds like fun," I said.

"It is. You know, it's tough being both parents for Annie most of the time. On Saturdays, it's our Girl's Day Out. We have a wonderful time together."

When we finally arrived back at my apartment, it was nearing midnight. I said, "Do you still have time to come in and have some pastry? I don't want to keep you out too late."

She said, "Are you kidding? I don't have a curfew tonight. I've got all the time in the world." She stopped before she barely got out her last word, and there was a look of shock on her face.

"Kelly? What's wrong? Was it something I said?"

Without a word, she pointed to my Miata. I turned to look, and saw that someone had taken a knife and completely shredded my convertible top.

TWELVE

∘ ∘ ∘

AS I got closer to my car, I could see that the knife the vandal had used was still embedded in the driver's seat. I started to open the door when Kelly grabbed my arm. "Wait a second, Ben; there might be fingerprints."

As I looked down through the ripped top, I said, "I doubt the killer's that stupid, Kelly."

It took her a second to realize I was talking about Jerry Sanger's murderer. "Do you honestly think this is related? Ben, this is probably just a sick, random act of violence."

I'd neglected to tell Kelly about the telephone threat I'd received the night before. In all honestly, I'd planned to tell her sometime, but it wasn't exactly second-date subject matter. After this, though, it was time to come clean. "I had a message waiting for me last night after our date. The point was pretty simple. Somebody told me to back off or suffer the consequences. It was a threat, and I didn't listen to it."

I could see her mind working as she took in the new information. Amazingly enough, she didn't scold me for withholding information from her. In fact, Kelly's only question was, "Did you tell the police?"

"Absolutely. I called Molly and told her about it as soon as I heard it on my answering machine. She took the tape, but I haven't heard anything else about it since."

Kelly took her cell phone out of her purse and punched in a few numbers.

"What are you doing?" I asked.

As she finished dialing, she said, "I'm calling the police. This has to be reported."

"Why don't you let me handle it myself." I could just hear Molly's reaction if I let Kelly report the vandalism to the police.

Kelly killed the connection and handed me her telephone. "So you talk to them; I don't care who makes the call. I'm not going anywhere."

I felt a wrenching in my stomach as I looked at my car, and a sudden increased desire to nail whoever was trying to scare me off my investigation.

Thankfully, Molly was at her desk late. "Hey, it's me. Somebody just cut up my Miata's ragtop."

"Where are you?" she asked.

"I'm in front of my apartment. Kelly Sheer's here with me."

"Don't touch anything. I'll be right there."

While we waited for Molly, I told Kelly, "Listen, I might as well tell you, she's not all that thrilled we're going out. I just thought I should say something to you if you wanted to take off before she shows up. I'll understand."

Kelly said, "I told you, Ben, I'm not going anywhere."

"Okay," I said. It felt like a lifetime, standing out there waiting for Molly to arrive. We both tried to start up a dozen conversations, but it was pretty obvious neither one of us was in any mood to talk. When Molly finally did show up, I would have been just as happy if she'd sent somebody else.

"I warned you about ragtops," Molly said as she surveyed the damage.

"Give me a break. Who could have seen this coming?" I asked. I wasn't in the mood for her attitude, not with my precious car violated by some maniac.

She spotted the blade imbedded in the seat. "Did you touch anything?"

"Not since we saw what had happened." Molly kept waiting for more of an explanation, but I wasn't about to give it to her.

She nodded, then said, "Okay, I'll have the car dusted for prints, not that it's going to do any good. I need you to hang around, though."

"We'll be upstairs if you need us," Kelly said.

Molly just shrugged, so we walked up to my apartment. Once we were there, Kelly said, "Well, that went well, didn't it?"

I hated to be put in the position of apologizing for Molly, especially since she was acting like a petulant child. "Kelly, I'm sorry. I'm not exactly sure why she's acting like this. We've both dated other people before, and we didn't have any trouble handling it."

Kelly said, "Maybe I'm more of a threat than she's used to."

I didn't know how to answer that, so I kept my mouth shut. Instead, I said, "Would you like coffee with our dessert?" I suddenly realized she still had the bag of treats in her hand.

She said, "You're probably going to think it's silly, but do you have any milk? It goes great with this pastry."

I looked inside the refrigerator. "I've got 2 percent, and a little half-and-half."

"Two percent's fine," she said.

I was edgy enough without adding coffee to the mix, so I poured myself some milk, too, and put both glasses beside the plates on the countertop. Kelly served the crisps, and after the first bite, I was hooked for life. "I can't believe how good this is."

"It should be illegal, shouldn't it? Annie makes me take her there every other weekend, she loves it so much."

"Let me place my order now and you can pick some up for me the next time you two go," I said.

The doorbell rang as were finishing our dessert, and Molly stood just outside.

"Come on in," I said.

"No thanks. I just need you to sign the police report and then I'll be out of your hair."

Kelly grabbed her coat. "Don't go on my account. I was just leaving."

I said, "Hang on a second, Kelly; I'll walk you to your car."

She said firmly, "I'm fine. I'll talk to you later, Ben." I'd been around enough women in my life to know that there wasn't any room for debate, so I let it go.

"Good night, then." It wasn't anywhere near the parting I'd been hoping for, and Molly's grin didn't help matters. In fact, her temporary look of triumph was enough to change my mind about accepting Kelly's departure gracefully. I turned to Molly and said, "You know what? I'll be right back."

I called out to Kelly, and she waited for me on the stairs, though I could tell she was a little exasperated with me. The crew that had gone over the Miata was gone, so we had the parking lot to ourselves. "What is it, Ben? Did you forget something?"

"Just this," I said, then gave her the decent good-night kiss I'd been looking forward to all day.

After we broke it off, she said, "I can't believe I left

without that. Thanks for reminding me," she added, laughing as we walked to her car. The tension between us had dissolved with the kiss, and while I'd known it was a risky move, I was glad I had decided to try anyway.

I took her hand in mine as we neared her Mercedes. "Listen, in spite of everything, I had a great time tonight."

"Me too," she said. I wrapped her up in my arms again and kissed her once more. After a minute, she said, "Ben, are things always this exciting around you?"

"Not until recently. So when may I see you again?"

Kelly frowned. "Annie's coming back home tomorrow, so my schedule's going to be a little tighter than it has been lately."

I wasn't about to let her go at that, not without at least trying again. "If you're worried about finding a babysitter, my Mom's already volunteered her services. You should know she's great with kids."

Kelly smiled. "Thanks, but I've got Mrs. Embry. She's great with Annie, but if I need a backup, I'll let you know. Seriously, I promised Annie we'd spend some girl time together when she gets back. Can I call you?"

"Just so you don't wait too long," I said.

As Kelly drove away, I wondered how things would change between us now that her daughter was back in town. I was going to pursue the chance to be with Kelly, but it was up to her to decide when and how Annie should be brought into our budding relationship. Until then, I fully understood her desire to keep her life with her daughter separate from her time with me, and I had no problem with her need to make her child the top priority in her life.

Molly called down from my door, "Are you going to keep me waiting here all night?"

"I'm on my way," I said, taking the stairs two at a time.

After I joined her inside, she said, "Ben, are you still digging into the murder?"

"I wouldn't say I'm doing all that much digging," I said, backpedaling. "But I have been asking a few innocent questions."

She gestured toward the parking lot. "I wouldn't call that an innocent response, would you? You've got to stop, and I mean right now."

I'd seen that serious set to her jaw enough to know that there was more going on than she was letting on. "What are you hiding, Molly? Is there something I don't know about?"

She paced around the room, starting to speak half a dozen times before she finally said, "You're not going to back off without a good reason, are you?"

"I honestly don't know. Why don't you give me one and we'll see."

"Ben, if you breathe a word of this to anyone, I'll have your hide. Do you read me?"

"Yes, Ma'am."

Molly said, "Okay. It's against my better judgment, but I'm going to trust you. It seems that Jerry Sanger was distributing more than just soapmaking supplies. I've got a hunch he was also wholesaling drugs."

"Drugs? You've got to be kidding me." Even with my low opinion of Jerry Sanger, I never dreamed he'd be involved in such a filthy business.

"I wish I were, but there are some things that don't add up. His standard of living was a great deal higher than anyone could expect, given his income. We got suspicious when we saw his bank balances and started taking a closer look at his real apartment. That place he took your sister to was not much more than a closet. His real place is pretty amazing. Sanger's storage closet reeked of peppermint, and at first I thought he'd just spilled some samples in there. Then I started thinking maybe it was a way to throw off the drug-sniffing dogs."

"So what did you find?"

She looked as sad as I'd seen her lately. "Enough drugs to prove it wasn't for personal use. Have you heard anything about this sideline of his?"

"I swear to you, I had no idea what he was into. Nobody in my family did either, I'd stake my life on it."

"How can you speak for all of them?" Molly asked. "I know you'all are close, but you can't know everything they know."

"I do when it involves something that important. Do you think we'd keep doing business with him if we had the slightest suspicion he was selling drugs? No way. I'm telling you. We didn't know."

"Yeah, I guess you're right there. Well, he was dealing it to somebody, and chances are it was along his route."

I remembered Monique's sudden urge to go poking around in her attic. The squirrel story had been thin, and certainly didn't match up with her having a gun by her side. "Try The Soap Bubble. Monique White was acting awfully strange when I saw her this afternoon. She was doing something in her attic scuttle when I walked in on her, and she pulled a gun on me before she knew who I was."

Molly said, "And you waited to tell me this now?"

"Hey, she said she had a squirrel problem. I'd check her hidey-hole before she has a chance to move anything."

Molly raced out, and I said, "Let me know what you find."

She paused long enough to say, "Oh, believe me, we're going to talk about this again soon. I've got to get a warrant, then round up a few deputies. That's going to take some time. Are you going to be up?"

"I will be now, no matter how late it gets. I don't suppose there's any chance I can go with you, is there?"

She didn't even have to stop to think about it. "Stay here. I mean it."

I popped some popcorn, flipped on the tube, and caught the middle of *Casablanca*. It was the best way I could think of to pass the time while I waited, something to distract me and keep me from hoping that by morning my sister would be out from under Molly's cloud of suspicion.

I hadn't meant to doze off, but I must have. A knock at the door woke me, and I wiped my eyes as I answered.

Molly looked mad enough to spit nails.

"What happened?"

"Her shop was clean, including the attic." Molly brushed some cobwebs from her sleeve as she added, "Nobody had been up there for six months, including squirrels. There was a layer of dust all around the scuttle. The mouth on that woman made me flinch, and I'm used to some rough language."

How could that be? "She was up to something, I'm telling you."

"Well, if she was, she had time to cover her tracks."

I couldn't imagine being wrong. "Were there any oil spills in her shop?"

Molly said, "No, the place was well scrubbed. We borrowed a drug dog from Charlotte, and even he drew a complete blank."

"I just don't get it," I said. "It doesn't make sense."

"And I'm telling you, there were no drugs there. Her place was clean."

I had another thought. "Are you going to check A Long Lost Soap, too? Heather Kent might be involved, if Monique's not."

Molly shook her head. "She's a college kid working part-time at her grandparents' shop. There's no way she could do anything under their noses without them knowing it. Are you accusing them now?"

"I'm not accusing anybody. Sanger had to be selling his drugs to somebody."

Molly said, "It looks like it probably wasn't on his route, though. It's a dead end from here."

I thought about it, trying to come up with some sign that I'd been right. "Then how do you explain my car top?"

"There's something else we haven't considered."

"What? I'm willing to listen to anything at this point."

"Have you thought about the fact that this might be because of your love life? You're dating Kelly Sheer, and I've heard there's an ex-husband who's not happy with the situation at all."

"How did you happen to just hear that?" I asked.

"Hey, it's a small town. Maybe that's what the voice warned you to back away from."

"Then they wasted their breath," I said. "Besides, it can't be Kelly's ex. He's had their daughter for the past few days."

She shrugged. "Okay then, it could have been a random act of vandalism, not related to this case at all."

"You can't believe that, Molly, or you wouldn't be telling me to back off yourself."

Molly said fiercely, "You don't know what you're messing with here, Ben. By sheer dumb luck you might be putting yourself in grave danger."

"I won't do anything stupid," I promised.

"If I could believe that, I'd sleep better at night than I have been lately. Maybe you should stay somewhere else for the next few nights."

"Come on, I'm a big boy, I can take care of myself."

Her laugh was a short bark. "Don't you believe that for one second. If somebody really wants to get to you, they will. You've got more family than the von Trapps. Go stay with one of them."

"I'm not leaving my apartment. I'm not afraid."

Molly just shook her head. "That's the problem; you should be. I wish I could post a guard on your door, but we can barely afford the patrols we run at night."

"You worry too much. I'll be fine. Thanks for coming by and bringing me up to date."

She got to the door, then said, "I truly am sorry about your car. I know how much it means to you."

"Thanks. I do appreciate that."

She tapped my chest, then said, "In the meantime, watch yourself."

"Don't worry about me, Molly."

"Then what else would I do with all my free time? Good night, Ben."

After she was gone, I was in no mood to go to sleep. I paced around the apartment, thinking about all the things that had happened lately, and more importantly, what they meant. The fact that Jerry Sanger had been into drugs bothered me a great deal, even given the fact that I didn't like him before I knew that. Monique's behavior was too odd to discount just because of the bump on her head and the assault in her store. If she was dealing the drugs Jerry was selling, could that explain the break-in? Then why hadn't the police found any evidence of drugs on the premises? She'd been up in that attic for more than squirrel patrol, I knew it in my gut, but Molly had been sure that her shop was clean. I'd mentioned Heather to Molly more out of possibility than belief, but she was a college student, so she probably had plenty of opportunities to sell to her classmates and even possibly her professors. Everyone on Jerry Sanger's route was suspect, even Melissa Higgins, though I couldn't see her dealing drugs any more than I could imagine the Kents doing it. It was a nasty business that had suddenly gotten nastier, and I didn't want to have anything to do with it. By the time I was ready to go to sleep, I'd almost decided to go along with Molly's advice and leave the investigation to the professionals. I was a soapmaker, not a cop. Each to his own expertise.

I hated driving the Miata with the slashed top and seat, but it was still better than taking the bus, or worse yet, borrowing a vehicle from one of my siblings. On the way in to Where There's Soap the next morning, I stopped off at Samantha Locke's office. She handled the insurance for the shop as well as our individual policies. Samantha, a tall, thin woman with jet-black hair and a ready smile, studied the slashed top and seat, then said, "Somebody's not too fond of you, Ben. Have you jilted any women lately?"

"No, my heart is pure," I said. Samantha and I had been friends a long time, long enough for us to tease each other every time we spoke, even under such wholly unpleasant circumstances.

"That's not the way I've been hearing it around town," she said. "So you finally got around to asking the lady lawyer out. How was your date the other night?"

Great, now my insurance agent knew about my love life. There were times when a small town was just a little too small for my taste. "Samantha, with four kids of your own, I thought you'd have more to do than keep track of my love life."

She smiled. "Oh, but you make a wonderful hobby. How's Molly taking it?"

"She's fine. You're not seriously asking if she was mad enough to do this, are you?"

"No, that's not what I meant at all. I was just kidding, but I shouldn't have been. Has she seen this?"

I handed Samantha a copy of the police report. "She came over last night."

Samantha took the paper, walked around the shredded top, then asked, "Anything else happen?"

"There's a slash in the driver's side seat, too."

She examined it, then nodded. "Okay, I don't suppose you've gotten any estimates yet, have you?"

"How many do I need?" I'd dreaded the prospect of going from shop to shop when I knew I would use Harry's place, no matter what the cost to me was. I'd known him since he'd run the Mazda dealership, and when he'd gone out on his own, I'd been one of the first folks in line. He was honest, fair, and friendly, and I sent everyone I could his way.

"Just take it to the Mazda place and one other."

"I want Auto Finesse to do the work."

She nodded. "Okay, then you can skip the dealership. Tell Harry to call me before he does anything, though. Your policy covers a rental, too, but I doubt you're going to find another Miata while yours is getting fixed."

"I'll struggle through it," I said. "Thanks, Samantha."

"For what?"

"For making this as painless as possible."

"Hey, that's why I'm here. Ben, if you made somebody mad enough to do this, you'd better watch your back."

"So I've been told. I'll see you later."

I dropped the car off at Harry's, and to my surprise, he had a loaner he was willing to rent to me. It was a '67 Mustang convertible, and though it needed a new paint job, the engine was in fine shape.

"This is a rental?" I'd asked.

Harry rubbed a hand through his thinning black hair. He'd been on a fitness jag lately, and I'd spotted him a few times walking around town on his lunch break. He smiled at me, then said, "Not usually, but I'm going to restore it, so I thought, why not let it go out for now? Take care of it though, will you?"

"You have my word. When can I expect the Miata back?"

"Give me a week," he said. I started to protest when I caught his grin. He added, "Or if everything goes right, I could probably get it back to you by tomorrow afternoon."

"That would be great."

I drove off in the Mustang, unused to all the space I had inside. The power was there, too, and for a moment of guilty thought I considered seeing what it would take to trade up to it once it was restored, but then I decided that the Miata was fine and I should be happy with what I had. There might be one plus I hadn't considered driving around town in the Mustang; nobody would know it was me. I might even be able to get through the day without someone threatening me or destroying my property. It was a noble goal, at any rate.

I realized I had more problems than my transportation when I got to the shop. From the look in Kate's eyes, I knew that something bad had happened to the Perkins family yet again.

THIRTEEN

∘ ∘ ∘

THIS can't be good," I said. "What's going on?"

Kate looked like she'd been crying. "You need to get over to Louisa's apartment right now."

I felt my heart go cold. "Did something happen to her?"

"No, but I'm really glad she's been staying with me. She went home to get a change of clothes this morning and found out somebody broke into her apartment while she was gone and wrecked the place."

When was my sister going to realize she had to stop taking reckless chances? "She shouldn't have gone by herself."

"She didn't. Jim went with her," Kate said. "We're not stupid, Ben; we weren't about to let her go by herself."

"I never said you were. You need to call Molly and have her meet me over there. I'm on my way."

As I rushed back to the car, she said, "Jim phoned her right after he called me here. She'll probably be there before you show up."

I raced to Louisa's apartment, wondering what had driven someone to come after the Perkins clan. I wasn't about to let Molly try to talk me into believing that this break-in was as random as she'd said my car vandalism had been. There was no way she was going to convince me that they both weren't related somehow to Jerry Sanger's death. I just wished I knew how. What pot had I stirred so hard that the killer had decided to come after Louisa, too? Monique was up to something, but did I really buy the possibility that she might be a murderer, no matter how foul her attitude could be? Heather Kent seemed too nice to have done it. The fact that I even included Melissa Higgins and John Labott in my list of suspects proved how desperate I'd become. I wanted Steve Erickson to be the one behind all of our turmoil, but I hadn't pressed Molly hard enough about him. It was time to have her dig into his background, to start checking his history like she'd been checking Louisa's.

When I got to my sister's place, Molly was already there. She was standing by the door when she saw me, and she waited to go in until I joined her.

"How'd they get in?" I asked. The door looked untouched.

"Louisa said her hide-a-key's gone from the flower bed. I didn't have the heart to lecture her about how crazy storing a key there was."

"She wouldn't listen to you on a good day. She's constantly losing her front door key."

Molly frowned at the open door. "Well, she's going to get to start over. I'm not going to leave until she promises to have the locks changed."

"I'll see to it myself," I said.

Molly said, "This is getting to be a disturbing trend, taking these calls at your homes and at work."

"You don't have to tell me, how do you think we feel about it? Have you been inside?"

"Not yet. I saw you coming and thought you might be able to calm your sister down enough so I could look around."

"She should be all right. Jim's with her," I said. "Let's go in."

A patrol officer met Molly just inside the door and brought her up to speed, but I was more interested in my sister at the moment. Louisa was in one corner, sitting in her sky chair without really looking at anyone or anything in particular. The chair was a bit of whimsy, hanging from the ceiling without any support on the ground, and I knew it was Louisa's favorite place to be. Jim stood beside her, close enough if she needed him, but still respecting her space. I nodded to my brother without a word, and he added his grim greeting back. I glanced around the apartment before I joined them. Somebody had done a real job on the place. The sofa cushions were shredded, a sight that reminded me of my convertible top. Drawer contents were scattered around the room, and I could see through the doorway that the bedroom was in an equal state of disrepair. It was going to take a cleaning crew forever to get the place back in order.

I joined Jim and Louisa as Molly scanned the room. "Is there anything missing?" I asked my sister.

It took Louisa a second to register that I was there. She got up from the chair and wrapped her arms around me, crying softly at first, but then elevating it to a full sob that shook her entire body. Jim just stood there, ever vigilant, watching and waiting for something he could do. He and Louisa had had their share of clashes over the years, but there was no doubt they loved each other. Still, it had always been hard for my brother to show his emotions, or deal with someone else showing theirs. I let Louisa cry herself out, then as she tapered off, I pulled away and brushed a strand of her hair out of her face. "It's going to be all right."

"I know. As far as I can tell, nothing was taken, and the things that were ruined can be replaced. I just feel so violated that someone would come in here and do this to my home." That brought on another crying jag, which stopped quicker than the first one had. Molly, finding a window of opportunity when Louisa was calm, walked over to us. "Have you had the chance to see if anything valuable has been taken?"

"Besides my sense of security?" she said. "That's the most precious thing this monster has taken."

"Besides that," Molly said.

"I don't think so." Louisa looked around, walked slowly from room to room, then said, "I really don't have all that much. My grandmother's necklace is still in the jewelry box. Wait a second." She checked her underwear drawer, a shallow opening that hadn't been disturbed. I was surprised by my sister's exotic taste in undergarments. I could have gone years without seeing her collection of thongs.

She pulled out two fifties from the bottom of the drawer. "My emergency money's still here. I don't understand it; did they do this out of sheer meanness?"

"No, but I think whatever they were looking for was bigger than what that drawer could hold." Molly took Louisa's hands in hers, a surprisingly gentle gesture. "I need to ask you something, and I need the truth. This is off the record, at least as much as I can keep it off."

"Should I call Kelly before you talk to her?" I asked.

Molly shot me a venomous look. "This doesn't concern you, Ben."

"You'd better believe it concerns me. She's my sister."

Molly shrugged, then turned back to Louisa. "It's up to you, but I'm asking you this as a friend."

Louisa said, "It's all right. Go ahead."

"Louisa, I'm not sure—"

My sister said, "Benjamin Perkins, we've known Molly

all our lives. What's gotten into you? I trust her." She turned to Molly and said, "What do you want to know?"

"Did you realize Jerry Sanger was dealing drugs?"

Louisa was stunned by the news. My sister was no actress; the concept was really shocking to her. "Drugs? I can't believe it. Are you sure? You've got to be mistaken."

"I'm sorry to be the one to tell you about it. We found the evidence in his apartment." She added softly, "His real apartment, not that place you used to meet him."

Louisa said, "So that's what you think the vandal was looking for in my apartment? Molly, I swear to you on all that's holy that I had no idea. If I had, do you honestly think I would keep dating him? You know me better than that."

Molly said, "I do, and that's what's been bothering me. Let me ask you this. Did Jerry ever ask you to hold anything for him? Say a package or a box that was mysterious in any way?"

"Never, I swear it. I can't believe it. I'm just finding out what a snake he was, but this?"

"So where does that leave us?" I asked.

Molly said, "You and Jim should take Louisa out for a cup of coffee. I'll have my crew through here in a heartbeat, then you can help her clean up."

I turned to my brother. "Jim, why don't you take Louisa over to The Hound Dog? I'll catch up in a few minutes. I want to talk to Molly." Fortunately my sister lived close enough to the shop and its environs to walk to the café. They left, and Molly said, "What's this about, Ben? I've got work to do."

It was clear she was trying to get rid of me, but I wasn't going to back down. "Have you looked at Steve Erickson in all in this? I told you what I heard at Suds."

Molly grabbed my arm and pulled me outside. "That's real nice, Ben, questioning me like I was a schoolkid in front of other cops. Are you trying to get on my bad side?"

"I have a right to know."

She shook her head. "When are you going to get it through your head that you don't have any rights in this thing? You have no standing in this investigation. None."

"My sister is standing enough."

She stared at me a few seconds, then let out a big sigh. "Ben, you're driving me nuts."

I waited, refusing to rise to her bait or start another fight.

Molly kicked at a piece of mulch on the sidewalk and finally said, "Of course we checked Erickson out. I looked into his alibi myself, and it holds up."

"So where was he when Sanger was killed?"

"I shouldn't tell you this, but I know you won't get off my back until I do. He was with someone."

People could be bribed or coerced into supplying alibis. I was going to have to hear more than that before I dropped him from my list. "Who? They could be lying for him."

Molly said softly, "I don't think the mayor's wife is willing to lie for anybody under these circumstances."

Why wasn't I surprised? "He's a real piece of work, isn't he?"

Molly said, "His adultery alibis him for the murder. He's a real prince, but it looks like he didn't kill Jerry Sanger."

"I don't believe her," I said.

"What you do or do not believe doesn't matter here. You weren't standing there when she broke down into tears. Now go have that coffee. I'm busy."

As I walked to The Hound Dog to meet up with Jim and Louisa, I wondered if Erickson really was alibied for the murder. It would take a strong motivation for the mayor's wife to expose herself like she had, but I had to wonder if Steve Erickson had some kind of leverage he was using on her.

I was still weighing the facts when I walked in, greeted by "Return to Sender" the way only Elvis could sing it.

"Could I have some coffee, Ruby?" I asked as I joined Jim and Louisa. They were already sipping theirs, each staring out the window as the urbanites walked past. Harper's Landing had grown over recent years, and there were barely enough apartments and houses going up to meet the demand. A great many folks had opted to stay in the city where the restaurants, nightclubs, and shops like ours were situated. Louisa often bragged that she didn't even need a car. She could walk everywhere she wanted to go. She still had the Jeep, though, and I knew giving it up would be losing too much freedom for her.

Jim asked, "Where do we stand with this?"

"Well, nothing valuable's been taken. At least that's something." I hastily amended the statement to add, "Nothing they can file in a police report, anyway. Right now they're treating it as just another random act of vandalism unless they find something else out."

"What do you mean, another?" Louisa asked.

"Oh, that's right, you haven't heard. Somebody slashed my convertible top last night, then drove a knife into the seat."

Louisa shivered. "What's this world coming to? First Jerry's murdered, then Monique's attacked in her own shop, your car gets vandalized, and my apartment is trashed. Is somebody going after soapmakers?"

I took a sip from the cup, then said, "Somebody's after something; I just wish I knew what it was." I stared into my coffee, then said, "They have to be related, it doesn't make sense otherwise. But how? What's the common thread, besides our businesses?"

Jim said, "It's got to be just that. There's nothing else."

I couldn't bring myself to believe that. "What, some madman has it in for cleanliness? No, all the strands of the web come back to the center, and that's Jerry Sanger and his life."

Jim shook his head. "I don't get it, and I'm not afraid to admit it. I was always better with my hands than figuring stuff like this out. Ben, we're counting on you to get to the bottom of this."

I took a sip of coffee, then said, "That's what's so frustrating. I don't have any real clues, and too many suspects without enough motive to kill him. It's impossible. No wonder Molly's been hitting so many dead ends."

Jim surprised me by patting my shoulder. He wasn't big on physical contact with any of us; he never had been. "You can do this. I believe in you, Ben."

Louisa echoed it with, "So do I."

"I just wish I had as much faith as you two did," I said as I stared out the window, watching as the people passed by. As we waited for Molly's crew to finish, Jim and I tried to engage Louisa in some kind of conversation, but she wasn't having any of it. Finally, after two refills, I felt like I was going to start climbing the walls. I slid a five under my saucer and said, "Let's get out of here."

Louisa asked, "Do you think they're finished yet?"

"If they're not, they soon will be. Jim and I will stick around and help you clean up."

"You don't have to do that," Louisa said meekly. The fire was nearly out of my sister's spirit.

Jim said, "Don't have to; want to."

We walked her back to her place. Molly was just finishing up. To our surprise, there was a crowd milling around outside Louisa's apartment. My family, in full force, was there waiting for us.

"What are you all doing here?" Louisa asked.

Mom took a step forward, hugged her, and said, "We've come to make things right. Molly gave me a quick look around when I got here. As soon as the police finish their investigation, we get started. While the ladies clean, the men will replace that destroyed sofa of yours and your bed."

Louisa averted her gaze as she admitted, "Mom, I can't afford anything new right now."

Our mother said, "Nonsense, I've got a perfectly good couch and love seat set going to waste in my living room. I've been meaning to replace it, but I haven't had a good excuse till now."

Louisa added meekly, "But what about the shop?"

"There are some things that are more important than Where There's Soap," my mother pronounced. "We are officially closed until we can get you back on your feet." She turned to me and added, "Your class has been postponed until tomorrow. I've already called everyone on the list."

I wasn't about to disagree. Louisa needed us, every last one of us, and that was exactly what she was going to get.

After Molly's crew left and she released the apartment, the Perkins clan swarmed all over the place. In an odd sort of way it was fun working with my mother, brothers, and sisters on something that wasn't related to Where There's Soap. There was a constant conversation running, a dialogue covering dozens of family memories. Somehow we got started on past vacations, and the women were still discussing a trip we'd all taken with Mom and Dad to Canada by the time Jim, Bob, Jeff, and I got back with the replacement sofa and love seat. It didn't exactly match Louisa's mod décor, but she had to have somewhere to sit, and whoever had broken in had done a number on her living room furniture. We had to replace the mattress, too, so until Louisa could get a new bed, we'd taken her old one from her room at the house. I'd thrown a poster of a kitten on top, just to tease her.

She pounced on it and said, "I can't believe you brought Fluffy!" She'd named the cat in the photo the second she'd brought the poster home, and I was surprised to see her tape it up inside her closet. She kissed my cheek and said, "You're nothing but a big softy inside, aren't you?"

"It was a joke," I protested, but it didn't do any good. My brothers jumped on the designation with glee, rubbing it in at every opportunity. By noon, it was tough to tell that Louisa's apartment had ever been disturbed. I said, "What about the locks?" I'd called the locksmith as soon as we went back inside together, and he'd promised he'd be there by twelve.

"Oh, we forgot to tell you," Cindy said. "He came while you guys were gone. She's got new keys and everything."

"No more hide-a-keys, okay?" I said. "Give one of us your spare and we'll keep it for you."

Louisa had gotten some of her fire back since that morning. "Honestly, Ben, I can take care of myself."

"I know you can. So do you want me to keep the spare, or do you want to give it to Mom?"

She ignored the request, but instead asked, "Is anyone else hungry? Suddenly I'm starving."

Mom said, "Never fear, I can have lunch ready for all of you in twenty minutes."

"Mom, let's all eat out," I said. "I'll even treat."

Mom said, "Save your money, big spender. I've got enough deli meats and cheeses for everyone back at the shop. We can eat, then open up right after lunch." She took Louisa's hand in hers and added, "Unless you need us here with you."

Louisa looked around. "No, the place looks fine. I'm not going to hang around here all afternoon by myself. I want to work, too."

Jeff asked, "Are you sure that's such a good idea? This has been kind of a shock."

Mom thunked his shoulder gently. "You heard your sister; if it's work she wants, work we've got. Now let's go."

"What about my class?" I asked Mom as we lingered behind with Louisa.

"It's too late to reschedule it now. They can come tomorrow. Tell you what, we'll give them a 10 percent discount on anything they buy after your session tomorrow. Will that appease them?"

"No doubt some of them will jump on it," I said. Getting any kind of discount from my mother meant more than receiving free products from other shops. I wondered if my class would realize just how special an offer they were going to be getting.

After lunch, we reopened Where There's Soap. I felt out of sorts without my class to teach and hoped that they'd all be able to show up the next day. It was the last session for the melt-and-pour method, and I had some interesting things to show them with layering and scent combinations. I decided to make more samples for them, not because I had to, but just because I enjoyed the process so much. There are some enthusiasts who look down on the melt-and-pour technique, but I found it flexible enough to allow lots of variations without being out of everyone's reach. I was adding a pearlescent red pigment to a second layer in my mold when Cindy walked into the classroom.

She looked surprised to find me in the classroom. "Hey, Mom cancelled your class, remember?"

"Well, I wanted to work up a few things before tomorrow."

She picked up a vial of lemon balm and tossed it between her hands as she spoke. "You really enjoy teaching, don't you?"

I took the bottle from her hand. "It's fun. You know, I thought I knew all there was to know about soapmaking, and then I taught my first class. It's amazing the kinds of questions you get, and how eager the students can be. You don't know what you're missing."

She looked around the room, then said, "Yeah, well,

you're good with people. I'm not comfortable standing in front of a class and telling them what to do."

"Cindy, don't think of it as lecturing." There had to be a way to convey the meaning behind what I was doing. A thought suddenly occurred to me. "Let me ask you something. If you knew the path to a beautiful garden, someplace really special, would you keep it to yourself, or would you want to share it?"

"It depends on who I'd have to share it with," she said.

"Let's say it's someone who desperately wants to see it, will respect it, in fact, may even tend it and make it more beautiful?"

"I'd show them, of course."

"Think of our classes like that. These folks come here entirely of their own volition wanting to learn. You've got skills in soapmaking you take for granted, since you're surrounded by all of us, but these are people who want a taste of what you know. It's so much fun watching them discover the talents within themselves."

"I don't know," she said. "You make it sound great, but I'm not sure I'd be all that good at it."

"Tell you what; why don't you sit in on my class tomorrow? You don't have to say a word. Just sit in the back and listen and observe. I think you'll be surprised."

"Maybe I will," she said, then headed out the door.

I knew Cindy wanted to find her station in our soapmaking family, but she was going to have to do it in her own way. She had more natural ability for scent combinations than I'd ever have, but I wanted her to experience the fun of teaching, too. There was more to the process than formulas and blends.

Maybe tomorrow I'd have a chance to lead her to a new garden myself.

FOURTEEN

o o o

BY the time Where There's Soap closed for the day, I found
myself at loose ends. How could it be that I was already
used to spending my free evenings with Kelly when we'd
just shared two dates? I fought the urge to call her, knowing
that she was getting reacquainted with her daughter after
an absence. Kelly had warned me that she was devoted to
Annie, that she'd made a pledge that her little girl's happi-
ness came before hers. I just hoped that didn't mean that
there wouldn't be any room for me in her life, too.

My youngest brother Jeff found me on the front porch
after everyone else was gone. "I thought you left," I said.

He joined me on the step. "No, there's not much to go
home to. Renee's in Raleigh on business this week, so I've
been hanging around the shop." Renee was my brother's
sometime girlfriend. They'd had a casual relationship
for years, and the matchmakers in the family had given
up long ago on them ever making it anything more

permanent. Mom was constantly holding Bob up to Jeff and Jim and me, pointing out that at least one Perkins man wasn't afraid to commit. Jeff's pattern with Renee did eerily match mine with Molly.

"You want to grab a bite to eat?" I said.

He looked surprised by the idea. "You mean you're not going out with Kelly? I thought you two were a thing now."

I shrugged. "We had two dates. That's it."

In a curt tone of voice, he said, "Hey, I didn't mean anything by it. If you're not going out with Kelly, you could always call Molly. I know she'd love to hear from you."

I stood and brushed off the seat of my pants. "Sorry, maybe the two of us hanging out wasn't such a good idea after all." He was starting to sound like the girls, and I didn't need that from one of my brothers.

"Hang on, Ben." He grabbed my pant leg and added, "Sit down, would you? I hate it when you tower over me like that."

I sat again, a little reluctantly, when Jeff admitted, "I guess I'm still smarting from my rejection."

"Renee blew you off? Why?"

Jeff shook his head. "Not Renee, Molly."

That was news to me. "So you finally asked her out. I'm sorry she said no."

He laughed sadly. "That makes two of us. Bob said it was time I did something about my crush. You won't believe this, but Molly even gave me that speech that I was too good a friend to risk messing things up with her. Oh, man, if I hear that line again, I'm going to scream."

I patted his shoulder. "You can still take Renee out."

Jeff nodded. "You know, I was probably out of line asking Molly out."

"Because of me? Don't sweat it."

Jeff said with a laugh, "Believe it or not, my world doesn't revolve around your life, Ben. I took a chance fouling things up with Renee for a pipe dream. It was pretty obvious the attraction was one-sided, you know? I'm beginning to think maybe Mom is right. How do you know when you've found the person you're supposed to spend the rest of your life with? Am I sitting around waiting for something that might not ever happen?"

Since Dad had died, I found myself having more of this type of conversation with my siblings. It had made me uncomfortable at first, but that still didn't stop me from giving advice whenever it was solicited. "Let me ask you something. If Renee decided to stay in Raleigh and live there so that you'd never see her again, could you bear to live with it?"

He shook his head. "You don't know her that well. She hates big cities, Ben. Before she left, she was fussing about how big Harper's Landing was getting."

"Don't be so literal, you nit. What if she decided to leave for good? How would you feel about it?"

He thought about it for quite awhile, then finally said, "I'd miss her, sure, but would I move there to be with her? You want to know the truth? I'm not even sure I'd make that three-hour drive to visit her more than a time or two. I guess I just got my answer, didn't I?"

The last thing I wanted was to be responsible for my brother breaking up with his girlfriend. Mom would never let me hear the end of it, and I could only imagine how my sisters would react. "You know what? You're probably asking the wrong brother. I'm no better off than you are. Why don't we both corner Bob and find out what his secret is?"

Jeff said, "It's not always that easy getting someone as sweet as his wife is to love you. He's the first to admit it; he got lucky when he found Jessica."

"There are plenty of rabbit's feet out there for us, too, but we're not going to make anything happen by wishing for it. Now let's go get something to eat. I'm starving."

He nodded. "Okay, but I won't dress up. The last time you dragged me out to dinner, I had to wear a tie."

"Is it my fault I want my baby brother to have a little culture in his life?"

"Actually, yes, it is."

I laughed. "Okay, no suits or ties, I promise. We can go to Bubba Brown's for some barbeque, or if you feel like it, I'll even drive to the Burger Barn in Trailorsville with you."

"No, it's not Tuesday or Thursday. I only go there on apple day." I had to agree; the greasy spoon had the best cooked apples I'd ever tasted. Mom had been insulted by the declaration once, and she'd struggled for years in vain to duplicate their fare, with varying degrees of failure that never quite matched the original.

"So you pick the spot," I said.

"Why don't we walk over to The Hound Dog? At least it's close, and it's cheap, too. I don't want to break you."

"Why not? I haven't heard an Elvis tune since breakfast."

As we walked to the nearby restaurant, Jeff said, "You know what? I've been thinking about what you said, and I've come to a decision. I believe it's time Renee and I had ourselves a long, serious talk."

"Hey, don't do anything crazy on my account. I was butting in when it was none of my business. You're not going to do anything stupid, are you?"

Jeff said, "You want to know the truth? I think she and I both realize we've just been treading water lately. It's time one of us had the courage to face the facts."

Great. I'd stepped into it again. "Just don't tell Mom who gave you the idea. She'll shoot me."

He said, "No promises there. You know how it is when you get under that microscope. She's relentless."

"You're preaching to the choir, brother." The restaurant was crowded and I made a move to sit at a free spot at the counter when Jeff grabbed my arm. "Hey, it looks like they're leaving over there."

A couple from the back booth slid out and Jeff headed for the table before they could make it to the cash register. Ruby was busy, as well as Garnet and Phyllis, her two waitresses on the night shift. I grabbed one of the gray tubs and bussed the table myself, leaving the tip between the salt and pepper shakers. After I wiped the table down, I dried it with a napkin, then put two place mats down, along with wrapped silverware.

I said with a smile, "My name's Bruno, and I'll be your server tonight."

Somebody poked me in the ribs from behind and said, "Sit down, Bruno, you're making a scene."

As I slid into the empty booth, I asked Ruby, "Do I get an employee discount since I had to clean my own table?"

Ruby cackled and shouted to Garnet, "He wants the employee discount, Garnet. Tell him what it is."

"All you can eat, as long as you pay full price," she laughed.

"Now how can I pass up an offer like that?"

"So what will you have?" she asked.

I had no idea, but Jeff was ready to order. "I'll have a bowl of the vegetable soup and a grilled cheese sandwich."

"Ah, the dinner of champions," Ruby said. "How about you, Slick?"

"You know what? Make it two. That actually sounds pretty good."

"Should I bring you some milk to go with it?" Ruby asked.

"Sweet tea, twice," I said, after Jeff nodded.

Ruby had just left to place our order when Jeff nudged me. "Well look who's here."

I turned to see Kelly walk in, with Annie dogging her

footsteps. I waved in their direction, and was secretly happy when Kelly brightened suddenly.

"Ask them to join us," Jeff said.

"I don't know if that's such a great idea. She wants to be with her daughter."

My brother gestured around the room. "Where are they going to sit, on the floor? I swear, sometimes you just like to make things harder for yourself, don't you?" Jeff stood, waved to Kelly, and called out, "Come join us. We've got plenty of room."

They walked over, and Jeff offered his hand to the little girl. "You must be Annie. I've heard so much about you. Any chance you'd be willing to sit with me? I don't bite, I've had all my shots, and I took a bath almost eight days ago."

Annie giggled and slid in beside Jeff. That left Kelly beside me. "Hi," I said lamely, wishing for the thousandth time I had my brother's glibness. It was easy for him to be witty, though. He wasn't under any pressure.

"Hello yourself," Kelly said.

"Hi, Annie," I said.

"Hello. You're probably Mr. Perkins, aren't you?"

"Please, call me Ben."

Kelly said, "Actually, I like Annie to call adults by their last names."

Jeff laughed. "Whew, thank goodness I'm not one of those." He held a hand out to Annie and said, "I'm his brother Jeff."

Annie giggled again. "I'm supposed to call you Mr. Perkins, too, Jeff."

"Annie," Kelly said, trying to hide the grin I saw fighting to escape.

"Sorry," she said, obviously not meaning it at all.

Ruby came over and said, "Now aren't the Perkins boys

being neighborly sharing their booth with two beautiful young ladies tonight?"

"We were glad to," I said, hating how wooden I was sounding.

Kelly must have understood, though. She reached under the table and squeezed my hand before releasing it.

"Now what are you all having tonight?" Ruby asked.

Annie asked, "What are you having, Jeff—I mean Mr. Perkins?"

"Vegetable soup and grilled cheese, but you wouldn't like it."

"Why not?"

Jeff said, "It's really just supposed to be for grown-ups. You probably don't even like grilled cheese sandwiches."

Annie said, "Are you kidding? That's what I always get."

After they ordered and Ruby left, I asked Annie, "So how was your visit with your dad?"

"I don't want to talk about it," Annie said, the storm clouds coming up quickly.

"Did I say something wrong?"

Kelly said, "Wade's got a new girlfriend, and Annie doesn't approve."

Annie said, "He shouldn't be going out with anybody. You two are married."

"Not anymore," Kelly said. "We've discussed this a thousand times."

Annie said, "You're not going out with anyone, and he shouldn't either."

"We'll talk about it more when we get home," Kelly said.

Annie rebutted, "You always say that, and we never do."

Jeff looked up and saw Ruby moving toward us with a heavily laden tray. "Looks like it's soup," he said.

I tried to make conversation through the meal, but my heart wasn't in it. It was pretty obvious Annie wasn't ready for either of her parents to start dating again, and while I couldn't care less what Kelly's ex was doing, her social calendar was of eminent concern to me.

Somehow, we managed to get through our meal. Kelly handed Annie the check, along with enough cash to cover it. The little girl asked, "Can I keep the change again?"

Kelly said, "Yes, I suppose so."

Jeff grabbed our bill and before I could protest, he said, "Dinner's on me, Ben. Come on, Annie, let's go get in line."

After they were gone, Kelly said, "Ben, I'm really sorry about this. Annie's been so upset since she came home that I thought bringing her here might cheer her up."

"She's not too keen on you dating, is she?"

Kelly said, "She has this delusion that her father and I are getting back together someday. No matter how hard I try to convince her that it's not happening, she won't believe me. I can sway a dozen people on a jury with my arguments, but my own daughter won't budge an inch."

"She's immune to you," I said. "So where does that leave us?" Suddenly I was dreading the answer, afraid I already knew it.

"She'll just have to get used to it," Kelly said.

"It's not going to be a welcome with open arms, is it?"

Kelly shook her head. "I'm afraid not. Listen, if it's not worth it to you, just say the word. I'll understand completely."

I looked at her and smiled. "I don't even have to think about that. Of course it's worth it."

She glanced at her daughter, saw that she was occupied with Jeff, then kissed me quickly. "Thanks, I think so, too."

Jeff and I walked them to their car, then we headed back to the shop on foot.

"That was fun," Jeff said. "I always liked Kelly."

"You were pretty charming to Annie, too. Thanks for setting the bar so high."

Jeff laughed. "Ben, you worry too much. I'm sure, in your own awkward and clumsy way, you can be just as charming."

I shoved him gently. "Wow, is there a compliment in there somewhere? You're being too kind."

"I try." Back at the shop, he said, "I hate to run out on you in your hour of need, but I'm reading a mystery I can't wait to get to the end of. I picked it up at Dying to Read the other day; it's about a candle shop. Pretty cool stuff. Good night, Ben."

"Night, Jeff."

Back at my apartment, I found myself restless, turning the television on and off a dozen times, reading the same paragraph three times before abandoning my book and finally staring out the window as the wind picked up outside. There was a heavy breeze coming in, causing the trees around my apartment to dance in their wake. It was the best show around, and I watched it until I fell asleep.

WITH the next morning free of business obligations until my afternoon class, I decided to visit the people on my suspect list to see if I could stir things up again. It had taken me forever to fall asleep, and when I'd finally managed to nod off, I kept coming in and out of consciousness. There was something nagging at me about how I'd found Jerry Sanger, but I couldn't put my finger on it.

After a long, hot shower and half a pot of coffee, I was ready to attack my day and start nosing around again. I planned to save Monique for last, though she was near the top of my list. I was probably just delaying the confrontation that would surely follow, but putting her last in line was the only way I'd get the nerve up to talk to anyone. Since Heather Kent's place was the farthest from home, I drove there first. The Mustang was responsive and a real joy to drive, but I missed my Miata and looked forward to picking it up later in the day. As I drove, I considered my suspects. I hated to throw Steve Erickson out of the mix, but Molly had been so certain of his alibi that I had to downgrade him to my B-list. Besides Monique and Heather, I also wanted to talk to Melissa Higgins and John Labott again. John's rivalry with Jerry could have extended past love into business, and I wondered if Melissa had been telling me the truth when she'd scoffed at dating the dead man, but clearly Heather and Monique were still at the top. I decided to push Heather a little harder when I got to her place, and I had a plan in my mind when I drove up to A Long Lost Soap.

Heather was out in front of the shop, taking snips of some of the herbs growing in a pretty border.

"Harvesting already?" I asked.

"I'm experimenting. Ben, what are you doing here? Don't you ever work in your own shop?"

"I just wanted to let you know that I'm getting close. I'm expecting the last bit of proof I need this evening."

She stared at me, waiting for me to continue, but I wasn't about to say another word. Her reaction had been slightly tense when I'd dropped my little bombshell, but she quickly snuffed it out and went back to snipping hyssop leaves.

"Good for you," she finally said. "Is that the only reason you came by?"

"I thought you'd like to know. Aren't you the least bit curious about what I know?" I asked.

"Ben, it's a shame about what happened to Jerry, but I'm not going to let it ruin my life. I've moved on, and you should, too."

What an odd reaction. I finally said, "I just thought you'd like to know."

She shrugged, then stood from her harvesting. "You

really should leave this to the police, Ben. Now if you'll excuse me, I've got a wonderful idea I want to try before my grandparents come home. They're due back tomorrow. I'm so excited to see them."

As I drove to Melissa's craft shop, I hoped I'd have a better reaction from her and the others on my list than I had from Heather. Was she playing it cool, or did she really not care what had happened to Jerry Sanger anymore? If she was guilty of the murder, she'd certainly mastered the art of hiding it.

Melissa was talking to John Labott when I arrived at her shop, and for a second it threw me off, finding two of my suspects huddled together like that. I immediately jumped to the conclusion that they were conspiring about something until I realized that he was one of her suppliers as well.

I had a fence to mend. "Hi, John. How are you doing?"

After he offered me a frosty nod, he said, "Melissa, I'll check your inventory in back and see how you're doing on your craft molds."

"That would be fine, John."

After he disappeared into the storage room, Melissa said, "My, you certainly have a way with people, don't you? If looks could kill, I'd be standing over your dead body right now."

"What can I say—it's a gift. I'm sorry to drop in on you, but I just wanted to let you know that I'm getting really close to solving Jerry Sanger's murder."

Melissa clapped. "Aren't you clever? So tell me, Ben, I'm dying to know, whodunit?"

"I'm not ready to say yet. I'll know for sure tonight."

"Well, be sure and call me with the results, I can't wait to hear. But not after ten. I need my beauty sleep, you know."

Had the whole world gone mad? I said, "Do you mind if I speak with John a minute?"

She waved a hand. "I don't mind a bit, but I'm not sure he's going to welcome your presence."

"I'll take my chances," I said as I walked into the storeroom.

I found him going through a few boxes on the floor. "John, I'm close to solving the murder. I'll know without a doubt tonight."

He didn't even look up at me as he snapped, "You just can't keep your nose out of it, can you? Do the police know what you're up to?"

"They're supporting my investigation," I said, one of the biggest bald-faced lies I'd told since I'd been in the third grade.

"I find that very hard to believe," he said. "Now if you'll excuse me, I need to get back to work."

As I left the shop, Melissa called out, "Don't forget to let me know who you unmask."

I needed to track Steve Erickson down before tackling Monique. I called his office and was surprised to hear that he'd taken a few days off. When I asked why, the dispatcher told me, "He said he needed to get away."

Now what did that mean? Was he trying to get away from the stress of the investigation, or had he lined up another tryst somewhere?

I was still chewing over the possibilities when I got to Monique's shop. She was building a new display in the window with sprigs of lavender and sage. A bandage still covered one corner of her forehead, and it was pretty obvious from her first words that her gratitude toward me had faded overnight.

"Ben, you are getting to be a real pest popping in here all the time. What do you want now?"

"I came by to tell you that I'm getting close to figuring out what really happened to Jerry Sanger, and what he was up to the day he was murdered."

The look of scorn on her face was apparent. "Oh, please, you couldn't win a game of Clue, let alone solve an actual crime."

"The police don't agree with you," I said, managing not to flinch at the lie.

"No doubt your lady friend is just humoring you," she said. "It's amazing what some women will do for love."

"I just thought you'd like to hear that I'll know without a doubt by tonight," I said.

"This is getting rather tiresome," she said as she turned her back on me and started rearranging packages on the shelves.

I left her store uncertain if I'd managed to stir up anything other than dust. Nobody seemed to care that I'd bluffed about solving the murder. Did that mean not one of the people I'd talked to was involved, or was the killer better at hiding guilt than I was at seeing through it? I probably wouldn't know until later that night. I'd done all I could for the moment, planting the seeds of doubt in their minds. Now all I could do was wait.

FIFTEEN

o o o

AFTER a quick lunch and a stab at the paperwork on my desk, I was ready to teach the final session of my soapmaking class. Cindy was already inside the classroom when I walked in.

"So you're going to take me up on my offer," I said. "Welcome to my class."

"Remember," she said, "I'm not teaching, I'm just here to observe."

"That's fine with me," I said as I got out the samples I'd made the day before.

After my class filed in, I said, "First, let me apologize for the cancellation yesterday. We had a family situation that needed to be addressed, and I appreciate your willingness to come back today. Because of your gracious understanding, I'm happy to say that we're offering a 20 percent discount on all your purchases today, so feel free to shop as long as you'd like after the class." Mom had said 10 percent, but I couldn't see myself offering it with a straight face. After all, how much could they buy? I saw Cindy's eyebrows go up, but I just grinned in reply. I added, "Before we get started, I'm happy to report that one of our students, Herbert Wilson, is recovering nicely from a slight heart attack." There were worried faces in the group, so I added, "Constance said that he was fussing at everyone in sight, a sure sign that Herbert is well on his way to a speedy recovery."

That brought relief, and I was happy to see a few smiles in the group.

I continued, "Today is graduation day. We're going to play with some of the more advanced techniques of the melt-and-pour method of soapmaking." I held up samples, explaining how each creation was achieved to the class. "This is a technique using pearlescence. See how it shines?" I picked up another bar and said, "This layering technique adds depth to the original tones. It really picks up the light." I held up a sample of light blue soap with a gray rod running through it. "This is easier than you might think, and I'll be showing you how to do this as well."

"Don't these things take time?" a woman named Carolyn asked from the back of the room.

"To a certain extent they do, but once you know the basics, the execution isn't all that hard. We've got the freezer to speed up the hardening process, and I think you'll be amazed by how easy these are to do."

I handed out the samples, then showed them the techniques I'd described. After I was finished, I said, "Now choose one of the methods and try it yourself. Remember, this is the fun part. Don't be afraid to play."

I was helping a woman named Stormy with a tricky layered pour when another student named Linda asked, "When are you going to be able to help me? This just isn't working like yours did."

"Sorry, I'll be there as soon as I can." I looked at Cindy, who shook her head. I lifted my eyebrows and kept staring, and she finally agreed. My sister was going to get a taste of hands-on teaching, whether she thought she was ready for it or not.

By the time I got Stormy on the right track with her pour, I glanced over at Cindy. The scowl was gone, replaced by an animated expression as she and Linda worked on a rod pour.

By the time the class was completed, everyone had tackled at least one difficult project and had mastered it, though with varying degrees of success. I said, "Remember, everything we've done here this week, you can do yourself at home. Soap makes a wonderful gift, and it's practical, so don't be afraid to play. And most important of all, have fun."

They actually applauded as I finished, and I responded with a bow at the waist.

As the group attacked the shop, Cindy came up to me. "That was a dirty, rotten trick."

I tried to look innocent. "What? I didn't do a thing."

"You made me help her. Don't try to deny it."

"Hey, you're the one who volunteered. So how did it feel?"

Cindy admitted, "It wasn't the most horrible experience of my life."

"So are you ready to teach the next class we have here?"

"Don't jump the gun, Ben." She played with a mold for a second, then said, "But I might be willing to give you a hand if you want me to. I wouldn't mind being your assistant, just as long as I don't have to do the actual teaching."

I hugged my baby sister, then said, "That would be great."

Kate popped in the door and said, "I hate to break up your bonding, but Mom heard about your discount, and she wants to talk to you."

Cindy said, "I told you she wouldn't be happy."

"She'll be fine," I said, wondering what I could say to her to ease the sting of the lecture I was about to get. I approached her, and before Mom could say a word, I said, "It was either that or give full refunds for the entire class. They were not at all happy about you cancelling on them."

Since we'd never postponed a class before, Mom hadn't even considered the possibility of refunds. "Twenty percent is good," she said. "I can live with that."

"That's why you're in charge."

She smiled slightly, then said, "Just wait, Mister, someday the headaches are going to be all yours."

"There you'll have a fight on your hands."

Stormy interrupted, calling me over to one of our most expensive kits. "Ben, is that discount good for everything?"

I said, "The entire inventory," as Mom nudged me gently.

I thought about picking up the telephone and calling Kelly after my class was over, but the idea of Annie answering intimidated me too much to try. It was amazing how I was letting a preteen so thoroughly dictate my social life, but I hadn't made all that great a first impression on her, and I wasn't eager to dig my hole any deeper. Jeff could no doubt get Annie's blessing immediately to date Kelly, but I lacked my youngest brother's glib manner.

Around closing time, I found Jeff and Jim in the plant studying a layout diagram. "What's that?" I asked.

"Bob has this great new idea to organize our production line, or so he thinks," Jim said.

"So what's wrong with the old way of doing things?" I asked.

Jeff grinned. "Let's see, what did he say? It's inefficient, it's wasteful, and it's old-fashioned. Does that cover it, Jim?"

"Don't forget dangerous," Jim added.

I nudged myself between two of my brothers and looked at the plans. "Do you all have any idea how much this is going to cost?"

Jeff said, "Bob swears it can be done on a shoestring, but he's going to have to convince Mom, even if we give it our approval."

I studied the diagram for a few more minutes, then said, "You know what? I think he's got a good idea here."

Jim said, "That's what we were afraid of. We both agree with you."

"So what's the problem?"

Jeff said, "Come on, Mom's going to shoot this down, and you know it. It's money we don't have to spend."

I rolled up the plans. "If you two don't think Bob would mind, why don't I show this to her myself?"

Jim grinned, a rare sight for my usually grumpy brother. "Why do you think we've been standing here the last half hour pretending to study this thing?"

"Thanks, guys, I appreciate the support."

Jeff said, "Hey, what's family for?"

I found Mom at the register going over the day's receipts. "Do you have a second?" I asked her.

"One minute," she said, holding up one hand as she punched the calculator with the other. I waited, watching my sisters restock the shelves the second the front door was locked. I'd been afraid Mom would make us stay open late given the loss of revenue from closing down the morning before, but it was business as usual for Where There's Soap.

Finally, she said, "Okay, what can I do for you?"

"Come on back to the production line. I need to show you something."

"None of the boys are hurt, are they?"

I was struck with sudden inspiration. If there was one thing Mom valued hands down above money, it was the safety of her children. I said, "They haven't been yet, but if things keep going the way they are, I wouldn't make any guarantees."

"What are you talking about, Ben?"

We walked back to the production line, and I noticed all three of my brothers were conspicuously absent. I rolled the plans out on a worktable and said, "Bob's come up with a solution to a dangerous problem that we've all been worrying about."

She looked shocked by the statement. "And no one came to me? You're not keeping secrets from me, are you, Ben?"

"No, Ma'am, but until we had a solution, there was no reason to bother you with it. Bob's proposing we change the arrangement of the production line, but I've got to warn you, it's going to cost some money."

She scolded, "What's money compared to your health? Show me what he's got in mind."

I gestured to the plans, then to the actual layout. Mom frowned, studied the diagram long enough to memorize it, then said, "Tell him I said to go ahead with it. Does he know how many days we'll be shut down?"

There was a notation on the back of the plan, but I'd purposely hidden it from view until Mom okayed the project. "Bob thinks it can be completely finished in two weeks," I said, overinflating the estimate. Before Mom could say a word, I added, "But I think we can do it in ten days."

Mom said, "You've got seven; that's the longest we can spare to have the line shut down."

Bob's true estimate was eight days. I wondered how she'd come so close. She said, "Work a little harder, you can do it. I believe in you boys."

"Good enough," I said. "We'll get started on it right away. We've got a good inventory; I checked it before I came to you with this, so we shouldn't feel the pinch."

She patted my cheek. "Safety always comes before profit in this family; remember that, Ben."

I nodded, then looked for my brothers to tell them the good news.

All three of them were in the break room, polishing off the last of the chocolate-iced brownies Mom had brought in that morning. "I hope you saved one for me," I said.

"Come on, what did she say?" Bob asked.

"You know, my memory's kind of fading. It must be my blood sugar. Now if there was only something I could eat to give me a little nudge."

Bob broke off half his brownie, with Jeff and Jim following suit, though Jim muttered something about blackmail under his breath as he made his offering.

I took a few bites, wiping out one of the donated sections, then said, "We can start tomorrow. There's only one problem."

Bob said, "Go ahead, drop the other shoe."

"We've got seven days instead of eight. Can we do it?"

Bob grinned. "I padded the estimate to give myself some wiggle room. Seven days should be just right." Bob finished off the last of his brownie, then added, "But how did Mom know that?"

"Listen, guys, if there's one thing you should know by now, it's that our mother's tough to slip anything by on."

Jim hit my shoulder. "But you just did, didn't you?"

"What can I say, I got lucky. So, does anybody want to go out and celebrate our renovation approval?"

Bob said, "You're kidding, right? I've got to get started right now, before she changes her mind. I'd better call Jessica and tell her I probably won't be home for a week. Wish me luck."

"Good luck," we said in unison as he headed for the telephone. Jim said, "I've got to cancel a date myself. Jeff, why don't you call in for a couple of pizzas? We're going

to be working nights for quite awhile." Jim slapped my
arm. "Hope this isn't going to interfere with your love life."

"Did I have one? I hadn't noticed. I can stay awhile, but
I've got some things I have to take care of tonight."

Bob walked back over to us and asked, "Like what?"

"Things are coming to a head with Jerry Sanger's murder investigation, and I've got to be free to move around for
a while."

Bob looked at Jim and Jeff, then said, "Do one of you
want to tell him, or should I?"

Jeff said, "By all means, you go ahead."

"Tell me what?" I asked, a sinking feeling crowding
into my gut.

Bob said, "It breaks my heart to say this, but you've
done your part. We figured if you could persuade Mom, we
could handle the rest of it on our own."

"So you're saying you don't need me?" I asked, feeling
more than a little hurt by my younger brothers' attitude.

"Oh, we need you, but you're doing something more important digging Louisa out of this mess. Once you find the
killer and get Molly to arrest him, we'd love to have your
help."

"Okay, I'll buy that," I said. "I've got a feeling I'll know
something pretty concrete by tonight."

I'D never been bait in a trap before, and the more I thought
about it, the less I liked it. What if one of my suspects decided to eliminate me before Molly could arrest them? I
didn't have a gun of my own. Just about the only weapon in
my apartment was a baseball bat I'd used one season years
ago playing with some of my brothers and friends. It didn't
feel like much protection, holding it while I sat alone in my
living room waiting for a killer to show up.

It was nearly impossible to keep myself from jumping

out of my skin with every car door's slam and every footstep outside. When the telephone rang at ten o'clock, I nearly fell out of my chair.

It was the last person I expected to hear from that night on the other end of the line.

"BEN, is this a bad time? I didn't wake you, did I?"

As she spoke, I felt the earlier tension drain away. "No, it's fine. Hi, Kelly, I wasn't expecting to hear from you so soon."

"I just got Annie to sleep. She's been wired since she came home from her father's. Wade didn't even enforce her bedtime, can you believe it?"

"No. I mean yes. Sorry."

Kelly's voice hardened. "Ben, is there someone there with you? Listen, I'm sorry, I didn't mean to interrupt."

"Wait! Don't hang up." I said it forcefully enough so she could hear me.

Kelly said, "You don't have to shout, I'm still here."

"I don't have a date; I've just been sitting here waiting."

"You mean for me to call?" Kelly asked, then laughed. "Oh yes, I'm sure you're just on pins and needles waiting to hear from me, aren't you? Sorry, my ego just got a little carried away. So what have you been waiting for?"

I thought about keeping my trap to myself, but I suddenly realized that it wasn't the smartest thing in the world, egging on a killer without any backup at all.

After I told her what I'd done with my list of suspects, I said, "Kelly, if anything happens to me tonight, tell Molly what I've done, would you?"

"Benjamin Perkins, have you lost your mind? I can't believe you're doing something so foolish."

"I didn't have any choice. I had to do it. Molly won't believe me; she still thinks Louisa had something to do

with Sanger's murder. I figured if I gave everybody a little
nudge, it might force one of them to act."

"I'm not going to debate the merits of your plan with
you, Ben. Hang up the phone this instant and call Molly."

I heard a knock on my door, then said, "It's too late.
Somebody's here."

"Ben, don't answer it!"

"I've got to," I said.

"Then don't hang up. At least I can hear who's after
you. Say their name if you can manage it. Be careful, Ben,
I don't want to lose you."

I laid the telephone down on my chair, out of the line of
sight of whoever was waiting on the other side of the door.
With my heart in my throat and the baseball bat in my
hand, I unlocked the door and opened it.

Sixteen

○ ○ ○

I nearly passed out when I saw that it was Molly. "Come on in," I said.

"It's kind of late for a game, isn't it?"

I threw the bat down on the chair, then picked up the phone. I said, "It's okay."

She said, "What do you mean? Who was it?"

"Molly's here."

Kelly said, "I don't know whether I should be relieved or upset. Are you two going out?"

"I told you what I was doing tonight. It's not a date, believe me."

Molly's eyebrows arched at that, and I realized I should have been a little more tactful than I'd been. "Listen, I'll call you tomorrow."

"I'm not going to be able to sleep now. I want to hear from you as soon as this is resolved. I don't care what time it is. Do you promise?"

"Okay, I'll talk to you later. Bye."

She said, "Good-bye. And Ben?"

"Yes?"

"Be careful."

"You know it."

After I hung up, Molly said, "I don't even have to ask, do I?"

"No, I guess not. You must be a mind reader. I was just getting ready to call you."

She frowned, then said, "What have you been up to now, Ben?"

"Hey, I'm one of the good guys, remember?"

Molly said, "Don't try to squirm out of it that easily. Give."

I told her what I'd done. After I was finished, she said, "That's just like you, baiting everybody without a clue who was behind all this."

"That's not fair. I've had more than my quota of clues, and I've shared every one of them with you."

Molly said, "I know, and I'm sorry if I've been hard-nosed about it. That's why I came by in the first place. I'm making a peace offering."

"I'm listening," I said.

"I thought you should know before it hit the papers or the news. We just arrested Monique White for the murder of Jerry Sanger."

"YOU'RE kidding," I said as I slumped back in my chair. I had my suspicions about Monique, but I hadn't expected Molly to believe me without more proof than I had. "What happened?"

"We gave her some time to get comfortable again, then we paid her another visit at her soap shop. I don't mind saying we had a devil of a time getting the second warrant, but we finally managed it. There was a small amount of drugs stashed away in the attic scuttle, just like you thought. She actually had bagged dust to spread around after you found her up there, can you believe that? I have to thank you for the tip, Ben, it really was helpful. She didn't have time to hide it this time."

"So what tied her to the murder?"

Molly said, "Circumstantial evidence, mostly. Monique cracked the second we found her stash. She admitted selling drugs to some of her high-society customers. Monique said the soap shop had been a real hobby for her at first, but in the end it was just a front. Oh, and she admitted to breaking into Louisa's apartment and trashing it before she shut up. She was looking for Jerry's stash, thinking he might have left it with her. She said she knew we'd been through his apartment, but Monique hadn't heard that we'd found Jerry's supply."

"What about my car?"

Molly nodded. "Yes, she admitted to that, too. She said you were nosing around so much, she had to do something to dissuade you."

"I suppose the mugging in her shop was faked, too."

Molly said, "No, that was real enough. One of her drug customers got agitated when Monique couldn't supply them anymore. She's turning over a list of her customers, trying to get a break on sentencing."

I sat there in stunned silence. It was still hard for me to see Monique as a killer. "I can't believe she confessed to killing Jerry."

Molly paused, then said, "It's funny, but that's about the only thing she didn't admit doing. Monique's probably trying to wriggle out of a murder charge, but we'll get her. Anyway, I thought you should know."

After Molly was gone, I telephoned Kelly at home.

Kelly said breathlessly, "I was beginning to think you weren't going to call. Do you think Molly's presence there might have scared off the bad guy?"

"It turns out it didn't matter. She just arrested Monique White for the murder."

Kelly said, "That's wonderful. Louisa's completely off the hook now."

"I guess so," I said.

"You don't sound too happy about it," Kelly said.

"I don't know, it was just a little too neat, don't you think? Plus, she never actually admitted to the murder, though she confessed to a host of other crimes."

"Come on, Ben, she most likely wants to wait and try to plead it out to a lesser count. That's what I'd do if I were her."

"Yeah, I guess that makes sense."

"Well, I'm happy for you. Have you called Louisa and told her the good news yet?"

"I owed you the first call. She's next on my list."

Kelly said, "Wow, I'm honored. Now hang up and call your sister. She needs to hear this good news fast."

"Okay, I'll do just that."

I walked around the room a few minutes before calling my sister. Kelly was probably right. Monique was just holding out for a better deal. That was the only reason I could come up with why she hadn't included murder on her list of crimes. I let myself start to relax a little, then I called my sister.

I was glad when I found her at Kate's house. "Hey, I've got some good news. They just arrested Monique White for killing Jerry Sanger. She confessed to trashing your apartment, too."

Louisa's whooping scream on the other end of the line nearly deafened me. "That's fantastic news," she said. "I'm in the clear."

"So are my other suspects." I remembered my raw treatment of John Labott. I was going to have to find a way to make it up to all the people I'd put through the ringer over this case. Helping John out would be easy enough.

"Sis, while I've got you on the telephone, there's something we should talk about."

"What's that?" she said.

"John Labott's had a crush on you forever, but he's too afraid to ask you out."

"John? Are you certain? Ben, he hardly speaks three words to me when he comes by the shop."

"Believe me, he told me himself. The thing is, he's too shy to ask you out."

Louisa was silent on the other end for some time, then said, "John Labott. Who would have figured? Thanks for the heads-up." She paused, then added, "Have you told Mom the news yet?"

"About John? She's probably noticed, too; not much gets past her."

"I'm talking about Monique," Louisa said.

"I had to call you first, didn't I?"

She laughed. "I'm glad you did. Let me call her, will you? I want to break the good news myself."

"That's fine."

Louisa said, "And Ben? Thank you."

"I didn't do all that much," I said.

"You did in my book. You're the best brother a girl could ever have."

"I'm telling the other guys you said that," I said.

She laughed. "Go ahead. I tell them all the time. Thanks, Ben, I love you."

"I love you, too, Louisa."

* * *

IT took forever for me to get to sleep, and when I did, I had the most horrendous dreams. For some reason, plants were chasing me through the shop, and not just little ones. These tendrils would have made a giant octopus proud. Every time I turned one way, they raced to cut me off before I could escape. I was cornered near the essential oils we kept in the shop when I woke up screaming.

It was one of those nights it was best I was sleeping alone.

By morning light, I was more exhausted than if I hadn't slept at all. After turning the coffeepot on, I set the shower-head to stinging needles and used just the cold water. It was a slap to my system, and after enduring a few minutes of it, I gently eased hot water into the mix.

As I dried off, I was glad for the one luxury I still allowed Mom to do for me. She was a big fan of hanging towels outside on the clothesline, and I didn't have the heart to make her stop doing mine once I moved out. There was a freshness to the coarse texture of the air-dried towels that I loved. Bob gave me a hard time about it, but I knew his wife Jessica still did the same thing for him.

After two cups of coffee and more eggs than I needed, I was ready to face the world again. I'd expected a sense of triumph when I finally managed to unmask the killer, but Molly had deprived me of the opportunity. Maybe if she'd let me join her on the raid I wouldn't be feeling so down about it, but that was asking too much, even of her.

It was time for my life, or whatever I led that resembled it, to get back to some semblance of order.

I found my brothers in a joyous mood when I walked into the shop. I'd forgotten all about the remodeling, but it appeared they'd been at work for hours.

"There he is, the man of the hour," Jeff said as I joined them.

Bob said, "Wow, who thought all those Nancy Drew books you used to read would finally pay off."

"It was Hardy Boys, and you know it. Kate was the one who liked Nancy Drew."

"Come on, Bro, I caught you reading them, too. Admit it, you always wanted to be a great detective, and now you've managed it."

"I don't know how you get that. Molly made the arrest all on her own."

Jim said, "She was after Louisa, and you know it. If you hadn't pushed Monique on her, she never would have twigged. You're a hero, Ben."

"So why don't I feel like one?"

Bob said, "Because your case is solved and now you have to help us. Grab a wrench, we're dismantling the line."

"You know what? Hard work is probably just what I need. Let me grab some coveralls first."

As I worked under Bob's direction, it felt good to be doing something useful with my hands again. I'd spent less and less time with my brothers on the line since I'd taken over teaching the soapmaking classes on the other side of the shop. It was all well and good to teach, but I loved the line, too. As we worked, there were jokes and taunts, curses at stubborn bolts, and more stories from my three brothers than I could have imagined. Some of their heroic exploits were strictly fantasy, and I did my best to top them. It reminded me of all that was good about coming from a big family.

Mom walked in just before lunch and saw the production line nearly torn down to the concrete floor.

Bob said, "Now before you panic, you've got to realize that I know where everything is."

"That's not nearly as important as knowing how it all goes back together again," Mom said.

"Hey, trust me; I've got a handle on this."

"I can only hope and pray."

Jim said, "You need to have faith in your sons."

"Faith I've got plenty of." She grabbed me, despite the grease on my overalls, and hugged me fiercely. One apron was going to need a serious cleaning before it went back into the rotation. She said, "Benjamin, you are everything I hoped you would be."

I didn't know what to say to that, but fortunately, my brothers filled the gap of silence for me.

Jeff said with mock petulance, "I always knew Ben was your favorite."

Bob said, "That's because she dropped him on his head when he was a baby. She's felt bad about it ever since."

Jim added, "Don't laugh, she dropped you, too."

Bob retorted, "Yeah? Well, she left you in the bathtub too long."

Mom released me and said, "Boys, I love you all equally, you know that, regardless of how you try your mother's patience."

"Yeah, we love you, too, Mom," Jeff said. "Now how about letting Ben get back to work. We don't have him back here too often, and we're going to take full advantage of it."

Mom said, "You boys have to eat sometime, don't you?"

Bob said, "I wish we could, but we've got too much work to do."

Jeff looked at Jim, then put his wrench down and said, "It's time to strike."

"You're right, little brother. Suddenly I've forgotten how to work a screwdriver. How about you, Ben?"

"Let me see, what's a wrench look like again?" fighting to hide my grin.

"This is mutiny," Bob muttered.

Mom said, "No, it's lunch. I'd invite you all to the break room, but I'm afraid you'd scare off our customers."

Jeff said, "Does that mean we don't get to eat after all?"

"Perish the thought. Louisa," she called out, and my sister walked in carrying a basket loaded with sandwiches. Behind her came Kate carrying a tray full of glasses and a huge jug of iced tea. Mom said, "It's Cindy's turn to watch the front. Now eat up, boys."

As we devoured the sandwiches and tea after dutifully washing up, Louisa joined me at the bench where I was sitting and said, "Ben, are you sure John likes me?"

"Absolutely," I said between bites.

"I don't know; I just don't see it."

I took a gulp of tea then said, "Do you really think he needs to come by the shop every week, when none of our other suppliers make it more than once a month?"

"You could be right," she said. "He's just never said anything." She paused, then added, "You know what? I might be wrong. He hemmed and hawed once about seeing a movie, but before I realized he was asking me out on a date, I'd turned him down. So why didn't he try again?"

"Maybe he's waiting for you to ask him," I said.

"He's in for a long wait then. I'm done with men. Finished. Kaput."

"Hey, I'm not saying you have to call him today, but he seems like a good guy. You should at least give him a chance."

"Sorry, I don't think it's going to happen. But speaking of love lives, how's yours going with Kelly?"

I stared at the last bit of sandwich in my hand, then I said, "If you would have asked me two days ago, I would have had a completely different answer. Now, with her daughter Annie back in town, I'm not so sure."

Louisa patted my arm. "Don't give up on her, Ben—she's worth the effort."

I shrugged, ate the last of my sandwich, then said, "I've got to get back to work."

Jeff overheard me, and said, "What about my siesta? You know I like to take a nap after I eat."

Bob said, "You can doze off while you're working."

"With all this racket going on?"

Jim said, "It's never stopped you before."

I told the ladies, "Thanks again for lunch."

"You're most welcome. We'll be back with dessert in a few hours."

We dove into the job with fresh spirits, despite Jeff's protests that he really needed his nap. I was feeling aches in places I'd forgotten I had, and I knew it was going to take more than a cold shower to get me moving the next day. Still, I managed to keep up with my younger brothers without slowing down too much. By the end of the day, we'd managed to pull everything off the old line and clean the individual parts.

I stared at the mess spread across the concrete floor and saw Bob studying the components of our line.

I said, "It looks like a bomb went off in here, doesn't it?"

He shook his head. "I wasn't lying, I know where everything is. To be honest with you, we're further along than I thought we'd be. You really made a difference today."

I stretched, hearing cracks and pops as I did so. "I'm glad I could help, but I'm not sure how much good I'm going to be tomorrow."

"You'll be fine. This was the worst of the grunt work. Tomorrow we start checking the parts and reassembling them. It's going to be a lot easier from here on out."

Jeff joined us and said, "Easier than today? I'm going to go play tennis after we finish up here."

Jim countered, "If you can manage that, you didn't work hard enough today." I was glad to see my brothers admitting to being sore and stiff, too.

Jeff said, "Okay, you want the truth? I'm going to go home, take a shower, and go straight to sleep. I'm too tired to even eat."

"Somebody call 911," Jim said.

Jeff waved a loose hand at us and said, "See you all in the morning."

I left, too, and realized the second I saw the Mustang sitting in the parking lot that I was supposed to pick up the Miata. I dialed Harry on my cell phone and told him I'd be in sometime the next day.

He said, "I knew it. You just can't part with the Mustang, is that it?"

"Something like that," I said. "Do you mind?"

"No, just take good care of it. I'm getting itchy having it out on rental, especially after what happened to your car. Renting you another ragtop probably wasn't the brightest thing I've ever done." He paused, then added, "If you have your heart set on keeping it, I guess I could make you some kind of deal on your Miata. It might be fun to drive now and then."

"As much as I appreciate the gesture, I think I'll stick with what I've got. Thanks for offering, though."

The obvious relief in his voice made me smile. He said, "Good enough. I'll see you first thing in the morning. Your car's as good as new. By the way, while I had it in here, I noticed that you were a thousand miles over your oil change, so I took care of that, too."

"Thanks, I've been meaning to, but I keep forgetting."

"Hey, no problem."

I drove the Mustang home, then took such a long shower that the hot water ran out, something I'd done only twice since moving in. Sleep came quickly, but it wasn't undisturbed. The plants were back in my dreams, with thicker tendrils than before. The nightmare unfolded the same way, though. When I got to the aisle with essential oils, it nearly got me, and I woke up in a cold sweat.

I just wished I knew what my subconscious was trying to tell me.

SEVENTEEN

∘ ∘ ∘

THE image of the leafy plant coming after me was still vividly in my mind when I woke up the next morning. It drove me crazy as I showered. I was nearly too stiff to move at first, but then my muscles loosened up under the hard spray. The dream haunted me as I ate, and I was still thinking about it as I drove to exchange cars with Harry.

"Here she is, better than new," he said as we swapped keys. "How'd the Mustang do for you?"

"I didn't know what to do with all that leg room," I admitted. "If I'd had it a week, you would have had to get a court order to get me to bring it back."

Harry nodded. "It's sweet, isn't it? I can't wait to get it finished."

I laughed. "Then you'll find another project to dive into. You always lose interest after they're restored, don't you?"

Harry shrugged. "That's the challenge, bringing them back from the edge. I found this one sitting under a tree rusting away in Hickory. It was too good to just let die like that."

I decided to park the Miata out in front of the soap shop, not wanting to lose sight of it during the day. I was probably being overprotective about it since Monique was now safely in jail, but it made me feel better having it where I could see it. I found Bob chalking the clean-swept floor of the assembly area when I walked in. Jim and Jeff were watching him in silence, nibbling on doughnuts and sipping coffee.

"What's up?"

Jeff whispered, "The great mind's at work. Grab a doughnut and join the gallery."

"No thanks, I already ate."

Jim said, "So did we, but Bob actually cracked open his wallet and paid for these himself. Are you going to let an opportunity like that go to waste?"

My brother Bob was notorious for his tightwad ways. I grabbed a doughnut, then said, "They taste better when somebody else is buying, don't they?"

Bob kept muttering to himself, erasing a line one place and redrawing it somewhere else.

I asked Jim, "How long do you think he'll be at it?"

"You know how he is when he gets like this. It could be hours."

I started for the door that connected the line area to the shop. "Hey, where are you going?" Jim asked.

"I've got some work to do upstairs. Come get me when you're ready for me."

I walked up toward my office, but hesitated when I got to the shelves filled with essential oils. It was just as it had been in my dreams, so real I could read the labels. I scanned the bottles, counting them off in my mind as I reached each one. There were vials of almond, castor, coconut, lemon balm, olive, and palm, the bottles went on and on. And then it hit me. I backed up to one of the bottles I'd passed by, grabbed it, and held it tightly in my hand. The oil I held had a common name, one we rarely used in the shop. I suddenly realized what my dreams had been trying to tell me. I knew who had really killed Jerry Sanger, and it hadn't been Monique White.

I rushed out the front door, forgetting to stop long enough to tell my brothers where I was going. I had to know if my hunch was right.

I found my suspect putting a FOR SALE sign in her store window, and I knew I'd guessed right.

"I didn't know you were actually serious about selling your business," I said.

She replied, "It's been getting too much for me, and to be honest with you, I'm in the mood to do something different."

I followed her inside, suddenly unsure of my hunch. No, I had to follow it through. It was the only way I'd know for sure what had really happened. One of the herbs found in Jerry's pant cuff hadn't gotten there by accident. Someone had left it there as a calling card, a way of admitting to the world exactly what she'd done.

It wasn't until I saw the name on the bottle again that I'd realized the leaf pattern was one I was familiar with. I can't imagine why it took me so long to see it.

The common name for lemon balm, one of the leaves found in Jerry Sanger's pant cuff, was Melissa.

I put the vial on her counter without saying a word. She stared at it a beat too long, then said, "What are you doing with that?"

"You were too smart for your own good," I said. "Leaving lemon balm on him was your marker, wasn't it?"

"Ben, have you been out in the sun too long? I don't have a clue as to what you're talking about."

"Save it, Melissa, I know. You had access to lye; my brother told me you leached it yourself. It must have been pretty strong, the way it burned him."

She hesitated, then her shoulders slumped. "I didn't mean to kill him. Honestly, it was an accident. I was just trying to frighten him."

I felt a wave of relief flood through me as she spoke. I had been right after all.

Melissa asked meekly, "What happens now?"

"We go over to Molly's office and you tell her everything. I'm sure she'll take it easy on you once you tell her the truth." I wasn't sure of that at all, but it had to help if Melissa came in and confessed on her own.

Melissa stared at me a few seconds, then said, "You never would have known if that tramp hadn't been selling drugs for him. You can't imagine how angry I was when I found out what he'd been doing behind my back."

"So you didn't kill him because of the drugs?"

Melissa snorted. "Come now, Ben, if I'd known he was involved in such a rotten business, I wouldn't have gone near him in the first place. He told me he loved me, and that was something I never thought I'd ever hear again. Then I found out about your sister. She had to pay, Ben, you see that, don't you?"

Her calm demeanor was slowly starting to fade. "Is that why you killed Jerry at our shop?"

Melissa said, "I followed him there and confronted him. He laughed at me. Can you imagine it? When he tried to get up the stairs to your shop, I blocked his way from the top. He fell; I swear I didn't mean to kill him."

"How did the lye get on him then?" I asked.

"I had some with me, but it was just supposed to be a threat. The lid came off accidentally. When it hit him, it sizzled! He tried to push past me and he tripped. Yes, that's exactly how it happened." Melissa was testing versions as fast as she could think them up, and I wondered if we'd ever know what had really happened.

She said, "But you're too smart for me, aren't you? I know when I've been beaten. It's over now, isn't it? Let me grab my purse and I'll go with you."

I should have been suspicious when she reached down behind the counter, but it never occurred to me that she would try anything, not when I had her dead to rights.

Instead of her purse, Melissa came up with a jar of lye in her hands; there was no mistaking it, and there would be no pretense this time of a lid coming undone by accident.

It was already off.

"Come on, Melissa, you don't want to do this."

She said, "Move away from the door, Ben. I don't want to hurt you, honestly I don't. This won't kill you, but it will give you a nasty burn."

I couldn't let her just walk past me. "They'll catch you, Melissa; you realize that, don't you?"

"Oh no, I'm much too clever for them to do that. I never should have left that balm on him, but someone had to know what I'd done, that I'd struck from love and not deceit."

She edged closer to the door, and I moved away. I knew what lye could do to flesh, and I was in no hurry to see a personal demonstration. I fully believed Molly would catch up with her before she could cross county lines.

I raised my hands, and Melissa said, "Honestly, I'm not going to hurt you unless you try to stop me." She pulled the telephone off the wall, then said, "Don't follow me, Ben. You'll regret it if you do. I promise you that."

"I wouldn't dream of it."

She was at the door when she paused and said, "You have one of those cellular telephones, don't you?"

I admitted it, and she held out her hand. "Let me have it."

She took my phone and threw it on the floor. I half expected her to douse it in lye, but instead she ground it under
her shoe.

"There, you won't be able to make any calls with it now."

She went out the door, and I started after her. I wanted
to keep an eye on where she was going. Melissa saw
me following her as she was halfway across the road. She
turned in anger and started back for me, brandishing the
lye and preparing to throw it on me as a floral delivery
truck struck her head-on. An image I'll never be able to
wipe from my mind was the jar of lye drenching her face
as Melissa flew past from the impact.

There was only one thing I could do. I went next door to
the pet groomer and borrowed his telephone. Then I did
something that I should have done as soon as I'd gotten an
inkling about what had really happened.

I called Molly and told her everything I'd just seen and
heard.

MOLLY was nicer to me than I had any reason to expect
when she showed up. The ambulance had arrived a few
minutes before she got there, but there was nothing anybody would ever be able to do for Melissa Higgins again.
I'd warned the EMTs about the lye, and they'd approached
her with suitable caution.

Molly watched them cart the body away, then said,
"You should have called me."

"I know that," I said. "It wasn't about being in danger; I
just had to know if I was right."

"And it could have killed you," she said.

"I'm sorry."

Molly said, "I know you are, and I shouldn't be beating
you up about it. What's done is done. You know, I'd like to

think I would have discovered this on my own, but I'm not so sure I would have been able to. I have to admit I was just starting to believe that Monique was telling the truth about not murdering Sanger. She was too ready and willing to admit enough things to make your skin crawl."

"It's kind of ironic, but if Jerry Sanger had just been a lothario and not a drug dealer, nobody would have ever found out what had really happened. I can't imagine how Melissa must have felt when we kept digging into his past."

"You're the one who kept digging," Molly said.

"You would have found the truth soon enough. You're good at it."

"The truth?" Molly mused. "I quit looking for the truth a long time ago. I deal with facts, with evidence, and with confessions. I'm willing to leave what's true and what's right to the philosophers and judges."

A white truck passed us as we talked. Molly said, "By the way, thanks for that."

"What are you talking about?"

"Everywhere I go now I see white trucks. It's like they're haunting me or something."

I didn't know what I could say to her. I had just added another ghost myself.

I headed back to Where There's Soap and told my family en masse what had really happened. No one could believe it at first, and Louisa broke down sobbing at the news. I felt like a heel telling her like I did. Mom, Cindy, and Kate wrapped her up in their arms and they comforted each other as only they could. Jeff, Bob, and Jim wanted me to see the new layout, albeit in chalk, no doubt trying to distract me, but I had a telephone call to make first.

Kelly's secretary put me right through, and I said, "I wanted you to hear it from me first."

Kelly said, "Sorry, but I was at the courthouse when the call came in. I found out fifteen minutes ago. Ben, are you all right?"

"I'm a little shaken by how close I came to getting a face full of lye, but I'll be fine."

"How did Louisa take the news about what really happened?"

"She started crying all over again, but she's in the middle of a sea of Perkins women, and that's more comfort than anybody can stand. She's going to be fine."

Kelly said, "If you're up to it, I'd like to take you to lunch today."

"Do you think Annie would approve?"

Kelly said, "I had a long talk with my daughter this morning before school, and we settled quite a few things."

I hesitated, then said, "She doesn't like me, does she?"

Kelly said, "Give her time, she'll come around. For now, can you be satisfied with knowing that I do, and quite a lot?"

"I guess that will have to do," I said, then matched Kelly's laugh.

She asked, "So are you free for lunch?"

"I'll pick you up in an hour," I said.

As I walked back from my office, I saw that Louisa had dried her tears, done some kind of magic with her makeup, and looked perfectly normal again.

"You look great," I said.

Louisa shrugged. "I've got to let go. Having everybody around helped."

"Listen, I'm taking Kelly out to lunch, but you're free to join us."

Louisa said, "Thanks for the offer, but no, I can't."

"What, are you worried about being the third wheel? We'd love to have you."

Louisa said, "No, that's not what I meant. I've got plans.

I made them this morning before . . . before everything happened, and it's too late to cancel now."

"So who will you be lunching with?"

"If you must know, John Labott's coming by."

"So he finally called you."

"Not exactly. I took the liberty of asking him out myself, and after he got over his surprise, he agreed." Louisa smiled as she added, "He wanted to make it breakfast, but I told him I couldn't face anyone that early in the morning." She glanced at her watch, then said, "In fact, if I'm going to get there in time, I should go right now." She kissed my cheek, then dabbed at her lipstick. "Thanks again, Ben. I'm going to be fine now."

"I know you are, and you're most welcome."

After Louisa was gone, Cindy approached me.

"Do you want to kiss me, too?"

"Hardly, but I would like to talk to you."

"What's up, littlest sister?"

Cindy said, "You've got another melt-and-pour class next week, don't you?"

"Absolutely. I'm counting on you to pitch in."

"I don't want to help," she said levelly.

"Come on, Cindy, don't back out on me now. You'll love it, trust me."

"I don't want to help," she repeated. "I'd rather teach the whole thing myself. On one condition, though."

"Anything, just name it," I said.

"You monitor me from the back, and jump in if I need you. It's the only way I'm going to have the nerve to do it."

I hugged her. "You'll be fine. I'm proud of you."

"Well, I haven't done anything yet."

"Don't kid yourself. Making the effort is half the battle."

I was feeling pretty good about the world again when I heard a familiar pair of bickering voices coming from the kit section.

"Herbert, you should be home resting."

"Constance, you heard the doctor, he told me I needed a new hobby to ease the stress in my life."

Constance said, "What stress? All you do is hang around the house all day."

"And you don't think that's stressful?" Herbert said.

Constance answered, "Shh, there he is."

They spotted me and walked over.

"We want a refund on the classes we missed," Herbert said.

Constance retorted, "Herbert Wilson, that's not what we agreed on at all. We want to take the class over. We'll pay for it, naturally."

"We'll pay for half," Herbert said. "We've got two classes coming to us."

That's when I realized that things at Where There's Soap were truly back to normal.

SOAPMAKING TIPS
FOR THE HOME HOBBYIST

○ ○ ○

SOAPMAKING is great fun to do. It is easy to master, and has the added benefit of producing something useful that's also very attractive. I like to start with the basic soapmaking kits readily available at craft and hobby centers. Don't forget, soapmaking is a good project to try with children and grandchildren, too. It's also an excellent way to make sure they wash up!

There are several basic ways to make soap at home. For this book, I've used the melt-and-pour method. It begins with a basic soap foundation and allows you to enhance it with colors, scents, abrasives, antioxidants, and more. By the time you've customized your own soap, you've got a result that is unique and your very own.

For example, lavender, clary sage, chamomile, tangerine, rose, and lemon verbena all help make a relaxing soap, while rosemary, peppermint, lemon, lime, and jasmine are good for energizing you. There's even a soap for insomnia, using chamomile, orange, and lavender. The possibilities are endless.

To begin making soap with the melt-and-pour method, melt the base in a pan on the stove top or in the microwave per instructions on the package. Once your base is melted, add the ingredients you want to make your own special soap.

Once the mixture is customized with scents and color, it is ready to pour into molds. There are many molds available in a variety of shapes.

Because this soap is transparent, it offers countless opportunities to play. Objects that are resistant to heat can be imbedded in the soap once it is poured into a mold. This makes it special fun for children as they use their soap to get to the prize inside. Hard plastic toys, seashells, even coins make good additions to your soap.

Remember, as with any craft, the most important thing is to let your imagination free and have fun!

The Candlemaking Mystery
series by

Tim Myers
Each book includes candlemaking tips!

At Wick's End

0-425-19460-4

Harrison Black has to learn the art of
candlemaking fast when he inherits his Great-Aunt
Belle's shop, At Wick's End. But when someone
breaks into the apartment Belle left him, Harrison
begins to suspect that her death may not have
been an accident.

Snuffed Out

0-425-19980-0

When the power goes out in Harrison Black's
candle shop, he find his tenant electrocuted.
Now, as the tenant's death starts to look like
murder, Harrison will burn the candle at both
ends to catch a killer.

**Available wherever books are sold or at
penguin.com**

The Lighthouse Inn mystery series
by

TIM MYERS

Innkeeping with Murder
0-425-18002-6

When a visitor is found dead at the top of the
lighthouse, Alex must solve the mystery and capture
the culprit before the next guest checks out.

Reservations for Murder
0-425-18525-7

Innkeeper Alex Winston discovers a new attraction
at the county fair—a corpse.

Murder Checks Inn
0-425-18858-2

The inn is hosting guests gathered to hear the
reading of a scandalous will. But the reading
comes to a dead stop when Alex Winston's
uncle is murdered.

Room for Murder
0-425-19310-1

Alex's two friends are finally tying the knot. Now
Alex has some loose ends to tie up when the
bride-to-be's ex turns up dead on the inn's property.

**AVAILABLE WHEREVER BOOKS ARE SOLD OR AT
PENGUIN.COM**

B178